GABRIELLE MARIE KOZAK

Trooper A2

"Little Trooper"

For my grandmother, in gratitude for her caring support.
For the friends who have stuck with me through thick and through thin.
And for my Guardian Angel.

Contents

prologue

"They hate me," the woman whispers, glancing from the small bundle in her lap to the crowd outside. The crowd is an angry one, carrying protest signs and yelling at the house's inhabitants. By the second-story window sit the woman and her husband. The first holds a little baby; the second watches the rioters carefully.

"They hate us," he returns, contradicting her lightly.

She smiles slightly, rocking the baby back and forth. He wails, and she turns her attention back to him.

He is a sweet little thing, perhaps two months old, wearing a white onesie as well as a small, purple jacket with the words Little Trooper embroidered on the collar. He has dark brown hair like his mother, and purple eyes as well. But his chin is undoubtedly like his father's—firm and sharp.

His mother's smile deepens, and she gently touches one of his chubby pink cheeks. The baby gurgles, delighted to have his mother's eyes on him.

But he doesn't get to keep the attention. The next instant, she is staring out the window again, her brow furrowed.

"It's my name they're shouting," she points out quietly.

The man shakes his head emphatically. "No, it isn't; it hasn't been your name for years." He stands up, closes the window, and starts pacing.

The young mother smiles grimly, but she doesn't reply. The baby is fussing again.

"That crowd might get violent," the father notes casually.

He is tall and muscular, with light blonde hair and deep, dark blue eyes. He looks as if he can definitely handle whatever the crowd might throw at him and his family.

His wife nods in agreement. "How'd they know we'd be leaving?" she wonders aloud.

He shrugs, a look of annoyance crossing his face. "I dunno. I dunno what they're trying to do by being here, anyway. Weren't they telling us to leave?" he asks himself, scowling. "And here we are, leaving."

"Sometimes I think—" the woman begins, then bites her lip.

Her husband glances at her and shakes his head quickly. "No. Don't say that."

"I'm sorry," she murmurs.

She is tall as well, though not quite as tall as he is, and her dark brown hair is somewhat past shoulder-length, her bangs held back in a light blue headband. She wears a light purple jacket that looks like it has seen better days, but also as if it suits her completely and will never be discarded. It is the same color as the baby's.

She speaks a few soft words to the frightened baby to hush him, meanwhile glancing over at the three suitcases that stand by the door. One is set apart from the other two, and something about her purple eyes changes as she looks at it.

"Are we still going ahead with the plan?" she asks, hastily dabbing at her eye with the back of her sleeve. She will not let anyone see her crying.

He nods tentatively, watching her. "Is that alright?" he asks in turn.

She does her best to nod bravely. "Yes."

"We can wait to go until they've left," he suggests quickly as she stands up with the baby.

She puts her little one over her shoulder, and pats his back gently. He makes some appreciative baby noises and spits up, but she uses a cloth to take care of that.

"No." She shakes her head at her husband, lifting the baby up in both hands.

He giggles. She turns, so her husband can't see the new tears forming in her eyes. "We should go now. Or not at all. But I don't want him growing up like this." "Him" in this case obviously refers to the baby.

Her husband nods, a hint of sadness coming to light in his blue eyes. "Then let's go. Moira won't care if we're early or not. She told me she was ready yesterday," he adds. He reaches out a hand for the first suitcase, then stops. "Baggage or baby?"

"I'll carry the baby," Violet Whyte, née Arnnu, responds, walking over to the door with her precious burden.

Conner Whyte nods and grabs the handles of two of the suitcases, opening the door and leading the way down the stairs into the living room. It is decidedly bare of any decoration or personalization; it looks as if the couple are moving out, which they are.

The clamor accelerates as he opens the door, but the crowd falls back to let him pass. He stares at all the cold, hateful faces sadly, realizing someone is behind this—who, he knows not.

"Alright, we're leaving," he shouts to them all, waiting for them to back away from the small car parked out front. Finally they do, and he gets the suitcases into the trunk.

Conner wasn't expected Violet to venture out on her own, but when he turns she is right there behind him, with their child. So that's why the crowd has suddenly gone quiet, Conner figures.

Violet hands him the warmly blanketed bundle. "You buckle him up," she tells him quickly, feeling the crowd's eyes on her. "I'll get the last suitcase."

"Vi—" Conner begins, but she is already heading back. He looks down at his son's face for a moment, and smiles. Then he opens the side door of the car and reaches across the seat to put the little one in the car seat. He sits down temporarily to buckle him. The baby starts crying, but Conner knows that once the car is started, the crying will stop.

Meanwhile Violet is dealing with some slight phobia of being stared at as she drags the third and final suitcase out the door and locks it behind her.

Her hands tremble slightly, and a look of disgust comes on her face. Why does she have nerves like this now? Five years ago, she couldn't have cared less about crowds. But then again, she's never had to face such walls of hate as she does now.

Someone is trying to ruin their family life, she thinks ruefully as she rejoins Conner in the car, sitting in the seat he had just been in as he moves to the driver's seat.

Violet is dimly aware of the crowd melting away to let them through, as well as the loud hum of the car engine. She glances down at the little one, who now becomes calm.

"I hope Moira likes him more than she likes me," Violet whispers pensively, more to herself than anyone else, as they back out of the driveway and get into

the road. She feels a sense of overwhelming relief, and then something of tragic sadness, as she buckles herself quickly.

"Huh?" Conner asks absently from the front seat.

"I hope Moira likes him more than she likes me," Violet repeats, louder this time. She holds out her finger to her son, who wraps his chubby little hand around it tightly. She smiles at him.

"Moira does like you, Vi," Conner insists, keeping his gaze straight ahead. "And she likes him too."

"If you say so," Violet shrugs.

She glances at the baby again, who is starting to fall asleep. Her face softens.

"Oh, Evolet. I'm going to miss you so much."

one

"How was the first day of school?"

"Oh, school was great. Aunt Moira, can I stay for soccer tomorrow? You'd have to pick me up at 6, I think. Or I could walk home."

He was tall for fourteen: a strong-looking, muscular boy with curly dark brown hair that ended unevenly at the nape of his neck. His chin and cheekbones were sharply angled, and his slightly overlarge ears stuck out noticeably from his face. His eyes were a deep, striking purple color. He wore blue runners, clean white socks, dark gray pants, ironed calico shirt, and a blue coat that looked outdated but also suited him perfectly.

He climbed into the passenger seat and slammed the door behind him, then pulled his backpack off his lap and dropped it onto the carpeted car floor by his feet. He glanced hopefully across the drink holder at his aunt, a light brunette with a chin like his. She looked about thirty-five, dressed in office work clothing.

"Actually, we're going out for dinner tomorrow, so I think not," Moira Whyte replied, starting the car engine. She switched the gear to drive, looking tentatively at her nephew. "Seat belt, Evolet," she reminded him with mock severity.

Evolet Whyte laughed mischievously, fished the seat belt from up by his right shoulder, and buckled it quickly as Moira pulled the car away from the curb.

"But you're not gonna crash," he protested nonetheless. "You never do."

"Oh?" Moira's eyebrows arched up.

"Mhmm," Evolet insisted, his purple eyes dancing as he tapped some buttons on the car controls to see the map. "Why are we going out for dinner?"

"We're going to meet some people," Moira returned vaguely, swatting his hand away from the controls. "Don't touch those; you'll distract me, and I'll crash—for the first time."

"Ha," the boy laughed, but he took his hands away. "Who are we going to meet?" he asked irrepressibly.

"Guess you'll find out," Moira replied, the corners of her mouth curving up in a ghost of a smile. "Do you have any homework?"

"Nah." Evolet shook his head. "We had some summer reading charts to fill out and a few assessment tests to complete, but I finished those while I was waiting for you. It's going to be another easy year," he added laughingly, grinning at his aunt.

She smiled back. "I expect all A's, young man," she teased.

He nodded seriously. "Really, though, it looks like it's going to be a breeze."

"What are your classmates like?" Moira wanted to know.

Evolet shrugged. "They all seem pretty nice, though I don't know a lot of them. There are only a few from last year. I think most of the people around me are going to be great people to know, though one is a pain." He laughed dismissively, but Moira wasn't convinced.

"Why?" she demanded.

"Oh, he thinks I'm girlish or something, I guess. Purple eyes," Evolet explained swiftly, without waiting for further interrogation. "But I don't care. I like 'em," he added with a mock heroic expression.

Moira laughed. "They suit you," she had to admit, but then she got serious again. "You're not going to get into a fight, are you, Evolet?" She sounded slightly worried.

"Of course I'm not." A scornful light came into Evolet's purple eyes. "I know I can beat the tar out of any of them or all of them together—I don't need to prove it!"

He laughed confidently, but ran his hands through his thick brown hair, a sign that he was thinking hard.

"Yeah, I know you can, but just don't." Moira's voice was still anxious.

"Oh, don't worry, I won't," Evolet hastened to assure her, his cheerful, boyish grin reappearing on his face as he took his hands out of his hair and stuffed them into his worn coat pockets. "Can I have any hints about who we're going to meet?" he asked curiously a few seconds later.

"'May I.' And no," Moira told him briefly, keeping her attention on the road ahead of them.

"Is it Aunt Niamh?" he asked inquisitively. "And Uncle Darek?"

"No." Moira shook her head.

"Aunts Erin and Joyce?" her nephew persisted.

"No" and Moira sighed in annoyance.

"Aunts Nina and Cloe?" He sounded desperate now. "Aunt Giulia? The cousins?"

"Stop guessing," Moira told him flatly.

"Lane?" Evolet continued pensively, thinking of his best friend Lane Evans, whose family had moved away from Annapolis the preceding summer. The two were emailing, of course, but Evolet was still missing him.

"Evolet." Moira spoke quietly, yet firmly.

The fourteen-year-old sighed, and gave up, distracting himself by playing with the window controls. Moira was just about to tell him to stop it, but he spoke up first. "Hey, Auntie, can I race you home?"

Moira pondered the question for a moment, watching the teenager cautiously out of the corner of her eye. This wasn't the first time she'd acceded to such a request, she considered, and running was a good outlet for the boy's energy that might otherwise be spent taking her car to pieces. So she decided in the affirmative.

"Okay, I guess. But next time you wanna do that, ask me at school," she told him, temporarily parking the car next to the curb in front of an ice cream shop.

Evolet gave a tortured gasp. "And can I get ice cream?" he begged, opening his hands pleadingly. "I have allowance left."

"Get one for me, too, then," Moira acquiesced, "and don't let it melt. I dare you."

He laughed, slamming his hand down on the unlock and bouncing out of the car. "Double-decker blue raspberry?"

"Don't be silly," Moira scoffed, "you know I'm on a diet. Vanilla sandwich."

"Okay." The teenager bowed low before slamming the car door and dashing toward the shop, laughing loudly. "Go ahead—you get a head start!" he shouted back generously, though Moira was already starting the car.

Evolet threw himself on the door handle frenziedly and jerked the door open, making the lady behind the counter look up as he made a dramatic entry, cartwheeling in and landing upright in front of the counter.

The young woman knew him, and she smiled as the teenager brushed off his clothes hurriedly and caught his breath. "The usual, I assume?"

"Yeah, and Aunt Cloe, please hurry, I gotta beat Aunt Moira home," Evolet pleaded. "And she wants an ice cream sandwich."

"They're in the freezer," Cloe Marwick gestured, grabbing a cone and holding it under the chocolate ice cream dispenser obligingly.

Her eyebrows shot up at the loud slap Evolet's sneakers made as he vaulted over the counter behind her. "There are other ways of getting to the freezer, you know," she noted disapprovingly, watching the cone fill up.

"Oh. Yeah. Sorry," Evolet apologized absently, smashing an empty ice cream sandwich box, tossing it accurately into the trash can, opening a new one, and grabbing a sandwich out of it. He dug around in his pockets for change, but Cloe's voice stopped him.

"You're fine," she told the boy. "Just make sure you beat Moira."

She wheeled around to hand him his ice cream cone. "And don't go climbing over my counters anymore," she added quickly, smiling.

His purple eyes lit up, and he flushed, grinning self-consciously. "Oh, thanks," he beamed, taking the cone and heading for the small swing-door between the counter and the wall.

"Hey, are we going out to dinner with you tomorrow?" Evolet asked abruptly as he headed for the door, quickly licking the first drip off his cone.

"Uhh, not that I know of," Cloe returned, sounding somewhat surprised.

"Oh, okay. Thanks again, and see you soon," Evolet finished, waving momentarily before disappearing out the door. It slammed shut behind him, and Cloe laughed.

two

oira's car was long gone when Evolet ran back outside, but he didn't hesitate a moment before he took off down the street, his worn sneakers beating a double-dutch tat-tat on the pavement that was warm in the August afternoon.

"Evolet!" someone called after him. It was one of his new classmates' voices.

Evolet threw a wave over his shoulder with the hand that held the ice cream sandwich tightly. "See ya tomorrow!" he yelled back, not slowing his pace one bit.

He turned suddenly to dash through a small neighborhood park, not caring that the children and parents there stared at him as if he was out of his mind when he jumped and sailed cleanly over the fence. To beat Aunt Moira and the car, he was depending on making the cleanest cut he could, back home.

The next five minutes found him leaping ditches, tight-roping the tiny strips of grass between backyards, dashing through crowded streets, and the like. Finally he came within sight of a small town house, painted a warm yellow color, with a row of tulips in front of the raised front porch.

Out of the corner of his eye, Evolet saw Moira's gray car driving up the street, and he doubled his speed, jumping up the front steps just as Moira parked her car.

She got out, holding her purse, to find the fourteen-year-old panting for breath and laughing uncontrollably at the same time. Moira smiled.

"It's melted!" she exclaimed when he came down the steps and presented her with her ice cream sandwich.

Evolet wiped a telltale brown stain away from his mouth, and his face drooped. "But Aunt Moira, my hands were sweaty!"

Moira laughed and rumpled his already-rumpled hair good-naturedly. But she realized the wind had already made its messiness worse, and she clicked her tongue.

"You need a haircut," she told him. "If we don't do it tonight, then we'll have to do it over the weekend." She frowned. "But you probably want it cut in time for dinner tomorrow, no?"

"Depends on who we're meeting," Evolet returned hintingly.

"Only—oh, no you don't," Moira glared mock-severely. "I told you to stop. Also, you need to wash your face—and dress nicely for school tomorrow, more nicely than usual. We're going straight to the meeting-place," she informed him, "and you need to look better than you usually do."

"What, we're meeting the President of the U.S.A.?" Evolet's lightly tanned face wrinkled in puzzlement.

"Maybe," Moira returned mysteriously.

She walked up the porch steps quickly, but Evolet's voice stopped her just as she was opening the door. "I beat you," he shouted gleefully.

Moira turned, and looked at him, smiling as she took in his ruddy face, his disheveled hair, his lively dancing purple eyes. "So you did," she admitted. "But I'll beat you inside," she added, her eyes twinkling as she stepped inside that very moment.

He laughed and followed her in, wiping off his slightly dirty sneakers on the mat. Moira made her way to the kitchen, where she dropped her purse on the counter and looked at the clock with a sigh. It was 4:32 PM. She had about an hour before she had to make dinner.

"Want help with anything?" Evolet came into the kitchen, grinning impishly.

She looked him over, and sighed despairingly. "Face. Hair. And you don't need your coat in the house."

Evolet nodded hastily, his youthful enthusiasm somewhat quenched for the moment. "Okay," he called after him, walking back into the hallway.

"And your room is a mess," Moira added loudly, chuckling. "We're having company this weekend."

The announcement elicited a heavy groan from Evolet, one Moira could hear three rooms away. She smiled to herself and walked back into the living room.

She paused, and glanced up at the mantel above the fireplace. There were a series of pictures there, all of them of Evolet. A few baby photos. That one of him at the very top of the tree in the backyard, the one that was so blurry because she couldn't get a close shot. His twelfth birthday party; he was with Lane in that one. The two had been literally inseparable. There was a place for one she hadn't printed out yet: Evolet dressed for his first day of high school.

That was where Evolet found her a few minutes later, standing in the kitchen doorway and staring at the living room mantel. He tiptoed in from another doorway, and followed his aunt's gaze to the pictures and then looked back at her.

He lost his characteristic, goofy smile and sighed subconsciously. Aunt Moira had been doing that a lot, staring at those pictures, or just staring at Evolet himself.

He wondered what had happened to make her so pensive. She always seemed somewhat preoccupied now, he remembered. She hadn't been like that before. It had started a few weeks ago, when that letter arrived from Iceland that she wouldn't let him read. And she'd been spending a lot more time with him recently. But he wished she wouldn't be so sad.

As if she sensed he was looking at her, she turned, and saw him, and smiled. He grinned back.

"Okay, you look presentable now," she nodded approvingly. "What about your bedroom?"

"Oh, yeah," Evolet remembered, and turned. "I'll be done in half an hour," he told her, marching down the hall reluctantly.

He heard her quick steps behind him. "I'll help," she offered, "and we can finish in fifteen minutes. I've got nothing to do right now, anyway."

"Thanks." Evolet grinned. His Aunt Moira was so much better at cleaning than he was. Probably because she was an adult. Adults were always better at that kind of stuff.

Still, his room wasn't *that* bad, he reflected ruefully as he opened the door to the room that Moira had said had once been his father's. Sure, there were three pairs of shoes on the floor by the door, and the bed wasn't made, and his reading chart was falling off the wall, but those were easily fixed. He dove for his shoes, tossing them accurately against the wall next to the door.

"Neatly," Moira spoke up from behind him, and Evolet grinned and put the pairs next to each other carefully, with the toes touching the wall baseboard.

Then he realized Moira was going over to the half-completed puzzle on the floor at the foot of his bed, and he cartwheeled over in a panic. "Nonono! Please—I'll finish it—"

"Okay, but you better hurry," Moira conceded. "We need space for another bed in here."

"Huh?" Evolet wondered aloud, grabbing a random puzzle piece off the floor and looking around for where it fit.

Moira swatted his hand gently. "No, not right now; we have to finish cleaning up first. And someone's going to be staying in here with you for a few days," she explained.

Evolet dropped the puzzle piece, and his eyebrows arched up. "'Someone'?" he echoed. "My age?" he added hopefully.

"Guess you'll find out," Moira winked. "Now let's see about that bed. And hurry, because you have to mow the lawn before dinner."

three

"I decided against spaghetti," Moira told Evolet as he came in through the kitchen door, his face all red from working in the autumn afternoon sun. The sun was setting now, in the west, dyeing the blue sky a rich orange color.

Evolet went straight to the sink, poured water over his hands, and straight-away wiped the sweat off his face. He got his hands wet again and slicked his thick bangs back.

"Oh?" the teenager commented, hunting for a glass in the cupboard. He leapt up to grab a tall gray cup, and turned on the tap again, moving the cup up and down impatiently as he waited for it to fill up.

"Yeah, seeing as we're going to Pervitto's tomorrow. So we're having chicken tonight instead." Moira paused to drop another piece of breaded chicken onto the skillet. It sizzled. "Set the table, will you?"

"How many plates?" Evolet joked.

Moira's eyebrows went up. "Two, of course. And forks, and knives."

"Okay," Evolet responded, grabbing the plates out of the cupboard and heading into the dining room with them. He was back a few seconds later to take the utensils out of one of the drawers in the kitchen.

"And you can put the fruit salad on there, too," Moira added before he left the room.

"Where?" Evolet looked around and saw the glass bowl on the counter. "Oh, there," he answered himself. "Honeydew! Yum!"

Ten minutes later found the two of them saying Grace and starting their meal. They ate at a smallish table; since Evolet could remember, it had always ever been just the two of them, excepting the times when they had company.

"Hey, did you used to go to school at the high school here in Annapolis?" Evolet asked after the first few bites. Moira's chicken was delicious.

"Yeah, I did. Why?" Moira returned cautiously.

"Just wondering." Evolet lapsed into silence for a few minutes, his brow furrowed pensively as he continued eating.

Moira smiled. "You haven't told me about school yet," she noted thoughtfully, tilting her head to the side slightly. "How are the teachers?"

"Oh, they're nice," Evolet told her vaguely. "Say, Aunt Moira, did Dad go to school here too?"

"Yeah. I thought I told you that," Moira frowned and gave up on the question of school. "Any problems with mowing?"

"Nah." Evolet shook his head quickly. "It's super easy."

Moira nodded, but she still didn't look quite convinced. "Be careful anyway. My brother almost lost a toe once, mowing."

"Who, Dad?" Evolet looked up with a genuinely interested light in his purple eyes.

Moira actually laughed. "No. Not Conner."

"You still haven't told me who Mom is, or what happened to them," Evolet continued, a hurt tone creeping into his voice. "Ain't I old enough yet?"

"'Am I.' And I don't know." Moira stared at her lap. "I just…"

Evolet watched her, surprised. Usually she just changed the topic when he brought up his parents, his parents that he'd never known. Aunt Moira had brought him up since he was so little he couldn't remember.

Evolet knew that Aunt Moira had had a brother—two of them, apparently—and one of their names was Conner Whyte. That was Evolet's dad's name. Evolet knew some things about him, like how Evolet's favorite coat used to be his dad's. And Moira dropped hints sometimes, about how Evolet had a strong will like his father, and there was something about the boy's face that reminded her of her brother. But her nephew still hadn't got the full story. And he wanted it.

"Did they die?" he asked softly.

"That's a really good question," Moira considered.

"Aunt Moira, please," Evolet pleaded despondently, seeing her eyes start to twinkle, a sign that she was back to her normal self—and on her guard as well. "You always tell me I don't need to know yet."

"Well, you didn't," Moira told him dryly.

"So, now—?" Evolet began hopefully.

Moira appeared to consider for a moment, but then she shook her head. "Not yet. I don't want to be the one to tell you."

Evolet sighed. "At least tell me Mom's name. And what they looked like."

"Evy," Moira called him by his baby name, "I've told you what they looked like at least a hundred times. And I told you your mother's name."

"You told me what it means," Evolet protested.

"Same thing," Moira shrugged.

"Well, tell me what they looked like again, anyway," Evolet insisted, a dreamy look coming into his purple eyes as he remembered days long past, days he had asked his aunt the same thing.

Moira sighed. "Your dad was tall."

"Taller than you," Evolet couldn't resist adding gleefully, watching the smile that always played over Moira's face when she spoke about her brother.

"Yes, taller than me. And we had the same color eyes," Moira continued. "But his hair was much lighter than mine. And he was really brave and strong." She stopped and moved her chicken around her plate thoughtfully.

"And Mom?" Evolet pressed.

"Your mom was tall and strong, too. She had eyes and hair like yours. And I think her favorite color was purple," Moira remembered.

"Did you like her?" Evolet wanted to know.

Moira's mouth opened and closed a couple of times as she stared at her chicken. "No. I'll be honest—I didn't like her. But you remind me of her so much I think I could manage to like her now," Moira admitted.

Evolet smiled. "That's great."

He felt like saying he wished his mother were still around, then, but he didn't, in case it might disturb Moira. So he devoted his attentions to finishing his supper. The two were quiet. They usually were after they talked about Evolet's parents.

four

He is dreaming. No, he is remembering. It is one of the first things he can remember.

He is in the backyard, Aunt Moira's backyard. He is about four, a chubby little rogue with a crown of long, dark brown curls that spill all over his face. Aunt Moira tries to neaten it enough for school. He protests indignantly, waving his little hands about.

"I was waiting for Mommy. You said Mommy'd come back when I was a big boy—someday."

"You aren't a big boy," Moira tells him flatly, brushing the dirt off the front of his green shirt. She has finally found him near the top of the tree in the backyard, and now they're going to be late for his first day of preschool.

"Yes I am," the little boy insists volubly. "Big boys go to school."

"Yeah, but—" Moira begins, but she is interrupted.

"And I want Mommy to come back," little Evolet proclaims heatedly. "Lane has a Mommy. I want one too."

"Well, does Lane have an aunt?" Moira asks discreetly.

"Mhmm." The obstinate head goes up and then down. "He has three. And a Mommy."

"But you have seven aunts. And Uncle Darek," Moira points out calmly, dragging him inside so she can wash his face.

"But they aren't real aunts, or uncle," Evolet wails as she splashes the cold water across his bark-smeared cheeks.

"Mommy will be back someday," Moira hastily changes the subject. "And for now you have to be a good boy, so that she'll be happy when she sees you."

"O—okay," the boy acquiesces doubtfully.

Finally they are in the car. Moira accidentally drops a card on the floor, but before she can pick it up, her agile nephew is already scrambling for it. He passes it up to her, beaming.

She takes it, and pats his head fondly before buckling him in. "Oh, Evolet. What would I ever do without you?"

* * *

Evolet sat up in bed, brushing his hand through his sweaty hair. For a moment the dream was vivid in his mind, but then it started to fade, as dreams always do. He wondered why he had been dreaming about that morning he'd gotten up early to wait and see if his mother would come.

He could barely even remember it. He'd been so little then, and he smiled as he remembered his youthful naiveté.

The fourteen-year-old glanced across his dark room to the clock, reading the glowing hands. It was almost six in the morning.

He sighed, wondering if he should try to go back to sleep. The sun was just rising, but he didn't have to get up until six-thirty.

"Oh joy," he whispered to the darkness around him, wishing he hadn't woken up. But if he went back to sleep now, he probably wouldn't wake up in time for school. And an early start to the day was better than a late one.

Sighing, Evolet threw his covers off and leapt out of bed to say his morning prayers. A few minutes later he was back on his feet. He glanced at his bed, and, remembering his aunt's warning that they'd be having company soon, took a few seconds to spread his blankets a bit more neatly. That done, he went to get changed.

Ten minutes later found him sitting on his bed, tying his sneakers on for the day. Evolet hated shoes that he had to tie, but they were the only kind he could actually run in, unless he had form-fitting boots—which he didn't. He reminded himself to put a pair on his Christmas list that year.

Scowling hard at a stubborn knot that wouldn't come undone, Evolet finally shrugged and ignored it, triple-tying his laces. Anything less than that usually came undone, he knew; and anything more was an intolerable annoyance to untie. Evolet looked at his shoes and decided he was ready for the day, whether that day would involve chaffing in a classroom, running a marathon, or scaling skyscrapers.

Evolet felt certain he would prefer the latter two possibilities to the first.

A whistle was on his lips as he headed for the door, pulling on his coat; he realized Moira was probably asleep, so he went out silently and cracked the door behind him.

He glanced at the door to Moira's room, closer to the front door; his keen ears detected no sound, and he drew the conclusion that she was indeed still sleeping.

With that in mind, Evolet went into the bathroom, and got his hands wet, running them through his hair before washing his face. He brushed his teeth quickly, re-adjusted his collar, and made his way out the front door.

The sun was just rising, bathing the city in rays of golden light. Evolet took a deep breath, letting the clean, fresh autumn morning air fill his lungs. He breathed out slowly, smiling slowly up at the quickly brightening sky.

* * *

Upon not finding Evolet in his room, Moira searched the house quickly, calling his name. He wasn't anywhere inside, so she stepped outside the front door and glanced around for a moment before shouting for her nephew.

Except she didn't shout for him right away, because she suddenly realized that on the pavement in front of her, with the shadow of the roof peak, was the silhouette of a boy, a shadow that the early sunlight amplified and made much larger than the boy himself.

"Evolet, I see you," she called out finally, still staring at the shadow. There was a boyish, youthful chuckle from the roof edge above her, and the shadow moved slightly, getting drastically shorter as the teenager started climbing down.

"Can we call it a sick day?" he asked inquisitively, affecting a cough. He dropped down the last few feet, landing on the pavement step of the front porch a few paces away from Moira.

She looked at him, noticing instantly that while he might have looked clean when he set out on his morning run, he looked very different now, what with his dusty shoes, dirt-smeared pants, half-unzipped coat, unfolded collar, sweaty face, and rumpled hair.

"Evolet, you've never been sick a day in your life," she retorted flatly, suppressing a smile.

He scuffed the ground. "But I twisted my foot."

"Well, does it hurt?" Moira's eyebrows went up.

"N—o—o," the boy admitted slowly, a grin breaking out on his face.

"Right, you have fifteen minutes to shower and change," Moira ordered briskly. "You better be in the car by then, young sir."

"Yes, ma'am!" As he dashed past her into the house, he suddenly saw something on the floor, and bent quickly, snatching it. "Is this yours?" he asked Moira a moment later, turning and holding out a small white button.

"Oh, yes, I was looking for that yesterday," Moira remembered. Smiling, she took the button. "I'll sew it...tomorrow. I didn't think I'd end up finding it at all. Oh, Evolet. What would I ever do without you?"

He smiled embarrassedly, flushing to the very roots of his thick, dark hair. "Don't worry, I'll always be there for you," he returned automatically. It was what he always replied to that question, which he heard quite often from Moira, as he was always eager to help out in whatever ways he could.

Moira grinned and brushed his bangs back meticulously. "Better hurry, or you'll be late to school and I'll be late to work," she warned him. "Your timer is ticking!"

* * *

"Hey, purple boy."

"Hey, jealous," Evolet murmured distractedly, not looking up from his schoolwork at the short, impatient-looking classmate behind him.

"Purple boy!" the other repeated angrily. "I'm talking to you! Yeah, *you*, Evolet Whyte!"

"Mhmm, and I'm talking to you, too." With a sigh of resignation, Evolet drew a circle around the option *D* on the paper on his desk and pushed his chair back, tilting it on the two back legs till the shorter boy came in view. "What do you want, Kai?"

It was during the ten minute break, and their teacher had left the classroom. Most of the other students were talking quietly—some not so quietly—and Evolet was working on a Previous Knowledge sheet that was due the next day. But Kai Lenon wouldn't leave him alone.

"I wanna know if you're coming to soccer tonight. 'Less you're scared that I'll beat you," Kai declared triumphantly, as a few classmates around him, his "gang," chortled at the blank expression on Evolet's face.

Evolet stared at him a moment longer and shrugged. "You're ignoring me, and we want an even number of players for soccer," Kai explained annoyedly. "We need one more. So?"

"'Cept I can't, 'cuz my Aunt said so," Evolet returned calmly.

"Maybe if you want even players you could keep the scores. Or get someone else to do it. I mean, you do look like you could use some running," he added helpfully. There were some chuckles from nearby, including from Kai's friends.

Kai ignored the remark, though his face did turn a bit redder. "What, you let your aunt boss you around?"

"You don't listen to your aunt?" Evolet clicked his tongue. "You kidding me, bro? That's dangerous."

"Maybe for a purple-eyed sissy like you," Kai snorted triumphantly. "What, your sisters beat you up?"

"Ain't got no sisters," Evolet pointed out languidly. "Have you? Do they beat *you* up?" He grinned cheerfully, letting his chair legs touch the floor. Then he tilted them up again, and let go again, and repeat, drumming out a ragged pattern on the tile floor.

"Nah, but I'm not a wimp," Kai told him confidently. "So, you coming to soccer? Or is your nasty aunt gonna make you stay home?"

The drumming pattern stopped, and Evolet glanced sharply at his classmate.

"Wanna race?" he asked him deliberately a few seconds later. There was a chorus of *ooo's*.

"Race?" Kai asked blankly.

Evolet nodded. "Mhmm. Race. I'm assuming you know how to run?" He kept his voice frigidly polite.

Kai laughed. "If you're too afraid to fight, then yeah, I'll race—purple boy."

Evolet bit his lip. "Okay. After school. I've got two minutes before my aunt'll be here to pick me up. And if you finish eating my dust in time—maybe you can meet my aunt. Just maybe."

Smirking, Kai opened his mouth to retort, but before he could, the bell rang, and the teacher came back in. But before the boy slid back into his seat, he couldn't resist whispering one last word to his victim—or so he thought Evolet was.

"Later!"

five

Moira drove slowly down the street to the Annapolis State High School, watching her unusually energetic nephew hightail it along the rooftops, with some unknown, much slower boy heading in the opposite direction on the ground, probably still on the first lap of a race.

She sighed as she parked the car along the curb.

Evolet jumped lightly down from a café roof to the pavement, with a crowd of gasping teenagers a few feet away. Moira heard them shouting his name and cheering for him, and she had to smile, though she was wondering why Evolet had decided to go all-out against an obviously slower kid. Probably this was a serious match.

She saw him grinning at his classmates as he wiped his hands on the front of his pants and headed for the car. A moment later he'd run around the fender and pulled the passenger door open.

"Hey, Aunt Moira," he greeted her, still just a bit out of breath from his run-climb.

"Hey, Evolet," she returned gravely. "What was the duel?"

"Oh, nothing." Evolet shrugged self-consciously. "I was hoping I'd be done by the time you got here."

"You don't usually clobber someone like that over nothing," Moira observed, her eyebrows arching up.

"I was avoiding a fight," Evolet explained. He stared out the window and wouldn't meet his aunt's eyes. "Like you always tell me to."

"I do that for a reason, you know," Moira responded gently, tapping his shoulder lightly before taking the car out of park.

Evolet's shoulders dropped slightly. "I know," he replied, his voice a bit gruff.

"What, is your voice changing already?" Moira teased, smiling and dropping the discussion about fighting. "Don't tell me you're so old so soon."

"Sure I am," Evolet returned, making his voice as low as he could, just for fun.

Moira swatted him playfully. "Yeah, right," she retorted, starting to drive the car away. She paused for a moment, and frowned, as she saw the kid Evolet had been racing finally arrive at the starting point, on the verge of collapse, and shake his fist at the boy.

Out of the corner of her eye, she saw Evolet grin back cheerfully, and Moira sighed silently. She hoped her nephew wasn't getting too worked up about anything.

"So, guess where we're going?" she hinted, bringing her foot down on the speed to get them away from the school as soon as possible.

Evolet ran his hands through his hair. "Well, you did tell me Aunt Giulia's place yesterday."

"Oh, you're right, so I did," Moira remembered. "Also, it's called Pervitto's," she corrected him.

Evolet emitted a long, drawn-out sigh. "Why does she call it that?" he demanded. "Why not Giulia's?"

"I dunno," Moira had to admit.

"Who are we meeting, anyway?" Evolet asked, a mischievous twinkle light in his eye.

Moira laughed. "You'll find out soon!"

"The suspense is killing me!" the fourteen-year-old complained, as he finally grabbed his seat belt and buckled it.

Moira gasped. She had been so preoccupied she'd forgotten to make sure—

"You didn't remind me," Evolet excused himself in a hurt voice.

"Don't be silly," Moira scoffed. "You're old enough to know better!"

The car was filled with the two's laughter. Laughter that told just how Evolet and his aunt got along.

* * *

"Evolet!" Giulia exclaimed upon seeing the boy and his aunt enter her restaurant an hour or so later. "Moira! *Cieli!* It is so good to see you again!" She hugged Moira and Evolet and kissed the both of them on both cheeks, profuse Italian-style. Evolet blushed a deep red, and other regular customers in the restaurant started chuckling among themselves.

"I thought I made a reservation." Moira bit her lip.

"Oh, you did," Giulia waved her hands dismissively, "but I didn't realize it was today. No matter; I've got extra tables as usual." She sighed heavily. "I always do. Except on Sundays," she added brightly. "Then they're *all* empty."

"But this is Thursday," Evolet pointed out, grinning.

"The boy has a head!" Giulia gaped with an expression of extreme shock, then chuckled and pushed the boy's bangs out of his embarrassed face. "Right. I have extra tables. You want a two-seater?" she asked Moira briefly. "No, no—three or four. I'll sit with you," she grinned.

"Actually... We need eight seats at least, then," Moira estimated.

Giulia paused her characteristic Italian optimism to glance seriously at Moira for the first time, and her jaw dropped.

"When?" was all she asked.

Moira glanced at the clock on the wall. "Fifteen minutes." Evolet followed her gaze, and discovered that the unknowns would be arriving at approximately five o'clock.

Meanwhile, Giulia showed Moira to a large, unoccupied table in the corner of the room, slightly away from the others. He jumped to attention when Moira called his name, and sat down tentatively next to her. It was the biggest table Evolet had sat at since his fourteenth birthday party, and it made him feel nervous.

"I—I'll be back," Giulia promised hurriedly, looking flustered, and turned and disappeared into the kitchen.

The teenage boy glanced at his aunt, a thoughtful, slightly perplexed frown on his face. His eyes had adjusted to the dim Italian restaurant lighting immediately, so he could already see her clearly. And what he saw clearly was an obviously masked, fake smile.

"Aunt Moira," he asked softly, "What's going on?"

But before Moira could reply, her face froze as she looked in the direction of the doorway. Evolet knew, even before he turned around to look as he heard the restaurant door opening, that the unknowns were arriving early.

It seemed the entire restaurant went still.

Evolet stared at the blank look on his aunt's face, and then, as she stood up slowly, he stood up as well and turned to look at the door, his heart pounding.

six

Evolet stared in shock at the five people who entered the restaurant. The first to enter, who was also the tallest—a real giant, who had to stoop to get through the doorway—was a strongly built, muscular man of perhaps thirty, perhaps thirty-three. He wore a dark, not-so-formal suit: black shoes, dark pants, and a dark brown jacket over his collared shirt. His light hair was neatly combed back, trimmed just behind the ears. His eyes were a deep, dark blue, and reminded Evolet instantly of his aunt's. So did the man's solid, sturdy chin. Evolet knew exactly who the man must be, and the boy's heart skipped a beat as his mouth dropped open in revelation.

The man held the door open for the others accompanying him, without a glance at the restaurant's patrons. The next to come was a young woman who was also quite tall, though not as tall as her husband. Her eyes were purple—the same hue as Evolet's. Her hair was the same dark brown, though her chin was sharper. She was also in amazingly good shape and was probably slightly older than her husband. She wore high, laced boots, a dark blue skirt, and a light blue blouse, over which she had a strange purple jacket with a belt.

She stepped a few feet into the restaurant to allow the others to come in behind her, stopped, and looked around with a clearly practiced eye. Her scrutiny stopped when she saw Evolet.

The two pairs of purple eyes locked, but Evolet broke away a few seconds later with an effort to take in the next and last three to enter the restaurant.

There were two girls, almost as tall as him and probably a couple of years younger. They were obviously identical twins, as their light brown hair—like Moira's—and dark blue eyes stated boldly. They were dressed identically as well, with boots of the same style as their mother's, except smaller, pleated hot pink skirts, white blouses, and light purple knit jackets. They stared at Evolet quite shyly, as if unsure what to think of him.

Then there was the youngest, a chunky boy of nine, who had his hands stuck in the pockets of his small leather jacket that fit him snugly. He gawked openly at Evolet out of light, crystal-clear blue eyes. Except for the jacket, he was dressed much like the taller man, who was obviously his father, and his hair was the same color, though he had his mother's chin. He took in Evolet coolly before glancing away deliberately.

"Conner and Violet Whyte!" came Giulia's hushed realization from the kitchen doorway, and Evolet's suspicions were confirmed, though he'd known from the instant he saw the adults that they didn't need any confirmation.

Conner Whyte closed the door behind him softly, and glanced around the restaurant, seemingly missing the table in the dark corner.

"Giulia—" he began.

"We're over here," Moira interrupted, waving her hand suddenly.

Conner saw them, and he led the way over, ignoring the curious stares of the people he passed, who'd stopped eating, with their forks literally held still halfway to their mouths. Violet followed with the three younger kids. They came up to the table, and chose seats silently, Violet sitting next to Moira.

Conner glanced at Evolet expectantly, and the boy moved a seat down, leaving a seat between himself and his aunt for his dad to take. One of the girls sat down on Evolet's other side, and the other two children went over to the other side of the table, the boy sitting next to his mother and the second girl sitting next to her younger brother. There was a very awkward silence as they sat down, but Conner and Evolet were still standing, facing each other.

Conner looked down at the tall, strong boy, his keen eyes taking in every detail. The rumpled brown hair. The uncertain, nervous purple eyes. The unconscious twitching of the boy's fingers, held stiffly at his sides. The chin, so like his father's, and the finely angled face, all hard-set as he stared back.

In turn, Evolet studied his father's face, which told him all he wanted to know. There was sadness there, and joy, and hope, and fulfillment of that hope. Memory of some deep tragedy. A lively sparkle that told of happiness finally found. Deep emotions, some of which Evolet's fourteen-year-old mind couldn't put names to. He caught his breath, as the realization hit him finally that this man was his dad, and that he was alive, and that he was right here, with Evolet, and—

And that he was unspeakably happy and proud to see Evolet.

Finally Conner spoke, in a quiet voice, a voice tremulous and shaken with emotion.

"Hi, Evolet."

Evolet was completely overwhelmed. He wanted to ask a million questions all at once, but all he could do at the moment was turn to his aunt and ask waveringly, "Aunt Moira, these people are supposed to be—?"

That was when Violet burst into tears. Obviously happy tears, but it was still somewhat disconcerting for Conner and the kids, who went silent. Moira sort of shrugged helplessly and patted Violet's back, which didn't help, so she ignored her and stood up, hugging her twin brother, now that she considered the initial introductions made.

"Conner—it's been forever, literally," she told him, trying to sound severe but only succeeding in sounding impossibly happy.

She started crying a bit herself, and Conner hugged her back so tightly she suddenly gasped something about her back, and Conner let go, a guilty expression coming over his face. Moira laughed herself to tears.

Meanwhile Violet had come around the table to hug her long-separated eldest, crying how much she'd missed him. Evolet stood there stiffly, embarrassed and as any fourteen-year-old boy would be when confronted with a happily crying mother for the first time, though his quickly-working mind was already sorting through the options and telling him there was only one.

This "Violet Whyte" was his mother. The prospect of it made him rigid in shock.

Finally things calmed down somewhat, and people sat back down, while Giulia came up and joined eagerly in the conversation that soon began between her, Moira, and Violet. Violet hurriedly introduced the three other children to Evolet.

The twelve-year-old twins—yes, they were twins—were Alison and Jasmine. The one who was smiling at him now was Jasmine, he realized, along with a burst of shock as he discovered he was going to like her. Alison—maybe not so much. She wasn't quite smiling, just a little smug smile as she watched him with an air of condescension. The little boy was Charles.

Conner put his hand down heavily on Evolet's shoulder, and the boy jumped and glanced back at his father. Conner smiled.

"You look just like I did when I was your age," he informed his eldest son, smiling proudly. Evolet's face turned redder than it already was, if that was even possible.

The four siblings stared shyly at each other, till finally Jasmine began the conversation with a remark about Evolet, though not addressed to him directly.

"Evolet is so lucky, with purple eyes like Mom!" she exclaimed enthusiastically. "He's the only one!" she added needlessly.

Evolet laughed self-consciously, but he didn't reply to that comment. He didn't need to. Jasmine's daring set the other two off.

"Evolet, we've been in Iceland!" Alison announced, her face finally breaking into a grin, though there was still a tinge of something in her face that made her look not so friendly as Jasmine. Evolet blinked at her and glanced at Jasmine again, who was sitting next to him. She was still smiling broadly at him.

"Yeah!" Charles chimed in. "Hey, Evolet, can I race you later?"

"Race?" Evolet returned, with an impassive expression not unlike Lenon's earlier that day. But Evolet had already forgotten all about that race, what with the climactic events now pouring down on him from every side.

"Mhmm," the nine-year-old nodded seriously. "I'll beat you."

But Jasmine had other ideas. "It's going to be dark outside by the time we're done," she predicted, glancing knowingly at the three talking women, "and you know Mom and Dad don't like us running around at night."

Alison opened her mouth to make a retort, obviously annoyed at her sister for some reason, but Conner spoke up before his daughter could.

"That's right." He cleared his throat. "Maybe you two can race tomorrow or something." His voice was getting stronger now, though it was still quiet.

"You won't beat him," Alison told her little brother coldly.

"Yes I will!" the nine-year-old insisted emphatically. Evolet gave a strained laugh.

"Why, you can't even beat me," Alison pointed out, her voice dripping scorn.

"I can beat Jaz," Charles persevered determinedly. "I beat her the other day. Didn't I, Jaz—?"

"I was being nice!" Jasmine interrupted heatedly, obviously intent on retaining some sort of a reputation with her older brother around.

This time Evolet really did laugh, though shakily.

"No you weren't," Charles shook his head doggedly. He smirked across the table at Evolet.

Evolet didn't really care. He wasn't interested in fighting or competing, except of course when his or his aunt's reputation demanded it, and certainly he wasn't interested in petty sibling arguments, having not grown up with any himself.

Besides, he was feeling completely overwhelmed, a sensation that only increased when his newfound siblings continued to bombard him with questions concerning his personal capabilities, questions he didn't answer. He began to lose consciousness of his surroundings as the dream-feeling intensified.

seven

But suddenly, what seemed hours later, Evolet heard a deeper voice, and jumped suddenly, realizing he'd been staring aimlessly at the wall behind Violet. Conner was talking to him.

"Huh?" he breathed.

"How are you?" Conner repeated.

Evolet was dimly conscious of Giulia getting up, saying she was going to get dinner for them all, and warning them that if they didn't eat it, it would be an offense to good Italian cooking.

"I—I'm okay," Evolet managed. "How are you?" he added abruptly.

Conner smiled at him. "I'm good," he replied simply.

"Dad," Evolet continued, gathering together courage from some unknown source. His voice choked on the word, one he'd never thought he'd say. "Dad, why—why—"

"Why did we leave you with Moira?" Conner had obviously been expecting the question, and Evolet nodded simply.

"It's somewhat hard to explain," Conner began, "but you might be old enough to understand. You've heard of the Purple Blitzkrieg, right? In 2024?"

Evolet nodded again, wordlessly. It was the year 2041 now, and he'd definitely heard mention of the Purple Blitzkrieg in history class before, though he'd had a dentist appointment the day the rest of the class had watched a documentary on it.

"Did Moira tell you anything?" Conner asked him hesitantly.

"Tell me anything?" Evolet echoed confusedly.

"I didn't," Moira broke in, glancing seriously at Conner. With Giulia gone, she and Violet had fallen silent, and now Jasmine, Alison, and Charles were quiet as well. "I left that all for you to tell him, Conner."

Conner sighed deeply, and ran his hand through his light blond hair, in an expression Evolet knew full well. "Well, Evolet," he went on, his voice quiet, "I was in that army. Not the American army—not for a while, at least. I was in the Violet Army."

Evolet's face froze as he stared at his father in disbelief. He had never heard anything of the Violet Army but that they had held a virtual reign of terror over Annapolis and the other cities they invaded in a short week's time, massacring policemen and military students, drugging the population, and other crimes that left a blemish on Annapolis history.

"It's not the way it seems," Conner hastened to assure him, seeing him sit up straight, stiff in shock. "I was—err—"

"My dad was the Violet Army commander," Violet broke in suddenly, and Conner glanced at her in consternation. She went on nonetheless. "The Army was named after me."

"How—what—" Evolet gasped in distress.

"Evolet, I—" Conner began, but Violet interrupted him.

"Don't blame yourself, Conner," she told her husband smoothly, still watching Evolet. "None of it was your fault. It was mine."

"Vi—" Conner interrupted, but there was a flame alight in her purple eyes that said she wasn't about to stop.

"Your dad snuck into one of our headquarters," Violet went on, unflinching. "He was sixteen at the time. So we tested our latest version of the T4 on him, and when it worked, well, we put him on LVED."

"T4?" Evolet had to ask. "LVED?"

"T4 is a superhuman injection," Conner explained quickly. "You, me, Vi, Charles, Jaz, Ali—we all have it in our blood. I'm sure you already know how you're abnormally strong." Here Moira interjected a nod. "And LVED: you know, the illegal sedative the Violet Army used?"

"Oh, yes," Evolet remembered. "So—?"

"So your dad was drugged into working for us," Violet concluded for him. "It's not his fault at all. Really, it's mine."

"Vi." Conner spoke up again, and this time Violet didn't interrupt him. "It's in the past. You joined the Americans, and ended the war. Don't horrify him. Let bygones be bygones. It's over."

"Except it wasn't," Violet contradicted him sharply. She fixed her stare on Evolet again. "Even five years after it was all over, when the—the other leaders were permanently dealt with—they let me go because I joined them— well—"

"People weren't going to let us stay," Conner explained. "So we had to leave. And we didn't take you with us because we didn't want you growing up like that. We thought it would always be like that. So we left you with Moira."

"But, Mom, Dad," Evolet broke in, his voice trembling, "why—why didn't you come back for me?" He looked around at his three siblings, who were avidly watching the grownups and Evolet talk.

"It wasn't just popular hostility," Conner admitted. "There were threats, too. We couldn't risk that they'd hurt you somehow."

"Who?" Evolet demanded.

His parents and Moira glanced at each other.

"We came back because they got caught. Or we hope they did. They admitted to it," Conner explained.

"Kerry Maughan...Hilton's brother?" Moira whispered, and Violet nodded to her.

"So that's why you finally came back," Evolet breathed. He studied the table, pushing his chair out slightly. "Fourteen years later. I'd like to see anyone hurt me *now*," he added vehemently.

"Yes, but you see, there's the other kids, too," Conner pointed out hesitantly, looking at Charles, who burst into indignant protest.

"But—" Evolet stammered.

He realized the others were watching him again. They all were. Jasmine— or Jaz, as her nickname seemed to be—seemed slightly anxious. Charles was still infuriated. And Alison was watching Evolet carefully. He got the uncomfortable feeling she was sizing him up.

He was so overwhelmed. With his parents coming back so suddenly like that. And telling him everything.

Why hadn't Moira told him any of this before?

"But what about *me?*" he finally forced out, trying to cover the sob in his voice.

Why hadn't they come back for him? *Didn't they love him?*

"Evolet, we do love you," Conner told him firmly, as if he could read his mind. He put his hand on Evolet's shoulder.

"But then why didn't you come back for me?" Evolet suddenly felt a wave of anger and disappointment, and he stood up, letting Conner's hand drop from his shoulder.

How could they say they loved him if they'd let him grow up with only his aunt?

"It was too dangerous," Conner began, but Evolet interrupted him.

"You didn't want me," he concluded, his voice getting more high-pitched than usual. "I bet you could've done it. You're supposed to be superhumans after all, aren't you?" he challenged forcefully, making the other restaurant patrons turn and stare. "You could have taken me with you if you wanted to!"

"Evolet," Violet spoke softly, but the teenager wasn't paying attention.

"I never knew my parents," he cried out, with all the frustration he'd felt over the years audible in his voice, the frustration that he'd vented on Moira's house when he was younger, the frustration he was now supposed to be old enough to hold in. "I didn't even know you were alive."

"Evolet." It was Moira's turn. But Evolet was past listening even to her.

"Why couldn't I have even just known?" he whispered. "Who my parents were? That maybe, at some point, I might have had a mom and dad who loved me?"

"Evolet, we *do* love you!" Violet exclaimed. "It was just too—"

Violet hadn't planned on stopping there, but the next instant the fourteen-year-old was running out of the restaurant. His chair fell backwards behind him. Violet drew breath in sharply, and Moira gasped.

"Evolet, come back here!" Conner's voice was sharp and commanding. But either Evolet was already out of earshot, or he wasn't listening.

Violet stood up. Conner shook his head.

"If we leave him alone, he'll come back," he told her quietly. "He won't be like that. I'm sure he's just overwhelmed."

"He is," Moira assured the two. "He hasn't had a tantrum like that since he was six."

"Evolet had tantrums?" Alison tittered, and Moira glanced over at her distractedly.

"Yes—I was of the impression that every child did?—Where's Jasmine?" she asked suddenly.

Everyone looked towards Jasmine's seat and realized with a burst of surprise that she wasn't in it.

"She must have gone after Evolet," Violet decided. "Jasmine *would* do that."

"I'll go after them," Moira decided, standing up.

Conner shook his head while Moira and Violet sat back down slowly. "I have a feeling Jaz can influence him better than we can right now." He smiled pensively. "After all, they're both children."

eight

He was standing on the very edge of the roof of what just happened to be a fifteen-story building in the high-rise section of the city. He was staring down at the quickly darkening streets.

Someone looking up from the dark street might have seen him and taken him for a maniac who had escaped from a mental institution, but even if Evolet was maniacal in some respects, he was far from any kind of insanity now. He was definitely way too busy contemplating the new turn life had taken to even accidentally lose his balance, which was why finally he sat down and dangled his legs, a hundred or so feet above the pavement below, to think the matter over.

Maybe it was unusual for any average person to deal with overwhelming emotions on city office building rooftops, but not for Evolet Whyte. In fact, rooftops were his favorite places to argue with himself. The rooftop society, as compared to the ground society, was virtually nonexistent. In fact, the quota was one to however many people there were on the globe, excluding himself, of course. Himself and the birds. But they didn't count; just now, at sunset, they were going to bed. And they didn't nest this high, anyway. There was just the occasional chirping from below.

His mind was so full that he would've gotten a headache if he could. His parents were alive. They—they'd come back for him—

They *did* want him, he realized suddenly, as his mind cleared. They did.

But it was still too much to take in at once, and he kept staring at the setting sun, watching as the light slowly drained from the sky. The turmoil in his head grew still.

Evolet focused on the facts that he knew. They were alive; they'd come back for him; they did love him after all.

He had parents!

And as that wonderful thought dawned on him, he heard a slight creaking noise on the roof slates behind him, and realized he wasn't alone anymore. Someone else was there with him.

Momentarily frightened, he jerked his head around to see who it was. Then he discovered it was one of the twins, and when she smiled sheepishly, he knew it was Jasmine.

"Sorry for following you, I just wanted to, umm, uhh..." She broke off the apologies when she saw his small smile.

"Hey Jasmine," Evolet said.

"It's Jaz," she grinned.

"Jaz" and he laughed, some of his nervousness melting away. "Like Jazzy?"

"Nah, that sounds like Ali," she retorted, pulling a face. Evolet laughed again, and so did she. But then she looked around, a look of anxiety crossing her face momentarily.

"You can do that stuff?" she inquired eagerly.

Evolet stared. "What stuff?"

Jasmine gestured vaguely, at the rooftops around and below them. "The superhero stuff. Like in movies. You can do that?"

"Uhh, yeah?" Evolet replied, somewhat surprised at the question, as that kind of thing was normal for him, and he would've expected it to be the same for his younger sister.

She looked distinctly impressed. "That's so cool. Dad prefers that we stay on the ground—he says going so high is dangerous, whether we're superhuman or not." She giggled. "But Mom loves it," she added as an afterthought.

Evolet's smile widened. "What are Mom and Dad like?" he asked quietly a few seconds later.

Moving carefully, Jasmine sat down a few feet away from him and the roof's edge. "Well... They're both nice, I guess. But Dad is more on the cautious side. He taught us school at our house in Iceland. Mom took care of the training."

"Training?" Evolet echoed.

Jasmine glanced sideways at him and leaned back on her elbows, staring up at the sky. "Yeah, training. Like running and stuff."

Evolet looked down at the dark streets below. Well, not that dark; there were streetlamps that shone down on it. But with that exception, and that of the car headlights that went by, as well as the few office windows that were lighted, it was dark. The sun was almost completely set by now.

Evolet was beginning to understand. It wasn't just that his parents and siblings had been in Iceland—they'd also home-schooled and done extensive training, it seemed. He wondered if all that was because of the threats. He tried to shake off the bit of jealousy that they'd had all that training and he hadn't.

But Jasmine had been shocked that he could climb the way he could, apparently, so maybe things weren't as bad after all.

"What can you do besides climb on roofs?" she was asking curiously.

"Oh, I dunno," Evolet shrugged. "Run, I guess. Oh, and—" He broke off, standing up, and walked easily along the edge of the roof. It might've seemed extremely stupid, but for Evolet it was completely normal and safe, and he was gratified to see Jasmine's mouth drop open in shock and admiration.

"Oh my! How do you do that!" she exclaimed.

"Practice makes perfect," Evolet jibed, sitting down again. But this time he sat down farther away from the edge and closer to his younger sister, and he started re-tying his shoe laces. Despite the three knots, he'd been doing just slightly too much running, climbing, and jumping today to ignore the state of his shoes any longer.

"And your—our aunt lets you just do this stuff?" Jasmine gawked.

Evolet looked slightly uncomfortable. "Well, I mean... She doesn't know about a lot of it," he had to admit. "But what she does know she thinks has got to be normal for a kid like me." He grinned.

Jasmine grinned as well. "You're so lucky," she told him. "So you chase bad guys around? Vigilante?"

"Are you kidding me?" Evolet asked incredulously. "Aunt Moira would *so* kill me if I did that. And what's worse, even if I didn't tell her—if it got in the news, she'd know immediately who it was!" The boy sighed.

"She seems nice, though," Jasmine pointed out thoughtfully.

"Oh, yeah, you bet she is," Evolet agreed emphatically.

"So..." Jasmine stopped looking at the sky and turned to her brother, a serious look on her face. "Are you gonna start living with us? Or are you gonna stay with Aunt Moira?"

Evolet froze. He hadn't thought about that at all. Jasmine watched him expectantly.

"I...I dunno," he said finally, losing all his newfound confidence. "I don't know."

"What's it like to be a normal kid?" she kept up the rapid fire of questions.

The boy blinked. "A normal kid?"

She nodded, as if her meaning was obvious. "You go to school. Have friends. Right?"

"Don't *you* have friends?" he asked, shocked.

Jasmine shrugged. "I guess. I made one at school today. Livia Parson. Do you know her?"

"Nope," Evolet returned. "So you're going to school now? Why'd you ask me about it, then?" he countered.

"I only started yesterday, and I'm not used to it," the twelve-year-old pointed out dryly. "Some of the kids think I'm weird. Ali tells them I am."

"Oh, so Ali isn't?" Evolet's face wrinkled in confusion.

"I guess not," Jasmine muttered. "But Ali thinks she's cool. Cooler than you even," she added dubiously.

"She doesn't know me," Evolet returned dismissively.

"Yeah, but we've known about you for years now. Aunt Moira sent us your high school picture yesterday," Jasmine added gleefully. "Really, it's cool how you look so much like Mom."

"You look like Aunt Moira," he noted, eyeing her thoughtfully. Secretly he beamed to hear he looked "so much like Mom."

His younger sister giggled. "I do?"

"Mhmm," Evolet insisted, but just then they heard a voice faintly calling them.

"Jasmine! Evolet!"

nine

"It's Dad," Jasmine realized, leaping to her feet. "Quick, let's get down."

"It's fine," Evolet muttered, watching her make her way to the fire escape.

Suddenly he whistled sharply. She was about to grab it and slide down.

"Jaz! That one's old. It won't hold our weight," he warned as she turned to look at him.

"What, then?" she asked crossly. "How do we get down?"

"We climb," Evolet told her shortly, grabbing the edge of the roof and lowering himself down. He swung uncertainly, ignoring the dizzying drop below, then found his footing on the windowsill of a—luckily—unused office.

"You're crazy," Jasmine muttered, standing above him and shaking her head.

"Don't look down," Evolet advised her belatedly. He let go from the roof with one hand, and felt the projecting bricks for a safe hold.

Jasmine shut her eyes. "No. I can't do this."

Evolet looked around briefly. "Then...how are you getting down?"

"I'm going to...call a fire truck," she decided, keeping her eyes shut tight as panic crept into her voice.

"Their ladders aren't tall enough," Evolet burst her bubble. He glanced up at her. "Hey, it's alright. I'll help you. Or I can smash the glass and pull you in. But that'll set off security."

"I don't wanna mess with security," the girl muttered.

She finally opened her eyes, and looked down again, this time not at the precipice but at her older brother's cheerful, encouraging face.

She hesitated. "Is it really safe?"

"For superkids, yeah." Evolet grinned—and let go of the roof.

He almost fell backwards off the windowsill, but regained balance just in time, grabbing ahold of some cables running along the edge of the building. He tested his weight on them. They seemed to hold firm.

He got a couple of feet down before glancing back up at Jasmine. "I can get Dad to help you," he suggested. "You shouldn't have come up if you didn't know how to get down."

She took a deep breath. "I'll do it."

* * *

Five minutes later found the pair running like crazy through the streets of Annapolis, back to the restaurant. They'd reached the ground uninjured and were now eager to discover what their parents wanted.

They found them standing outside the restaurant.

"You guys didn't eat." Moira frowned at them. Jasmine sort of shrugged it off, but Evolet looked somewhat guilty.

"It's time to go, anyway," Conner noted, glancing hard at Evolet.

Evolet looked back, and then did something he'd never thought he would. He ran forward and hugged his parents tightly. And he felt his eyes watering. He'd never dreamed he could ever do this.

Violet lost her composure again, and hugged him and Conner both.

"Oh, Evolet. I missed you so much."

* * *

Evolet's drive home with Moira was unusually quiet. He was gathering his thoughts and emotions, figuring out how to organize them and adjust to the new facts that had been dumped on him. Moira was just quiet. Perhaps she, too, was thinking about her brother and his family.

But finally, about halfway through the long drive home, Evolet spoke up with the question that had filled his mind for so many years.

"Aunt Moira, why didn't you tell me?"

His voice wasn't shaky or sensitive now; it was her nephew's ordinarily strong voice. She glanced at him momentarily before turning her attention back to the dark road, and was gratified to see that he looked recovered.

She opened her mouth to respond, but suddenly gunshots rang out.

The car's left windows tinkled, one after another, the sound followed by crinkling on the right side, as projectiles sped through the glass and narrowly missed the car's passengers. The car lurched as Moira slammed her foot on the brake and ducked, shouting in surprise. Evolet yelled something unintelligible.

"Get down!" Moira yelled to him, recovering herself and hitting the accelerator again.

The car shot forward, but only momentarily, as more gunshots were heard and one or two of the tires were punctured. The car's wheels squealed to a stop.

"Evolet, get down," Moira told her nephew urgently, leaning below the window level in case there was further shooting. Her fingers trembled as she unlocked her cellphone.

"I am," the fourteen-year-old whispered back, crouched down behind her driver's seat. He hunched down, his back to the door.

Listening intently, his sharp ears detected running footsteps on the pavement.

Suddenly the window above him was smashed, and Evolet covered his head as the shards fell down on him.

Something was thrust through the hole, and Evolet looked up, his face bleeding. There was a gun stuck through the window, aimed down at him, held by whoever was their attacker.

Evolet caught his breath and ignored the bleeding cut on his face as he reached up slowly towards the gun. He leaned out slightly, and turned his head, glancing out the window at the attacker. Except not the face of the attacker, because the actual face was masked.

"Moira Whyte," the attacker hissed through the mask. "Where is Violet staying?"

Evolet discerned that it was a man's voice, and not just that, but also that the man was high-strung and fighting with some strong emotion. Repressing a smile, Evolet kept his careful fingers creeping up toward the weapon.

"V—Violet?" Moira gasped out. She had turned around, and was watching Evolet in a panic, her face white as she mouthed the words *Don't do anything.*

Evolet's fingers paused, and he looked hard at his aunt's tense face. Then his purple eyes shifted back to the aggressor.

"You know," the masked man snapped, obviously trying to disguise his voice. "Violet Arnnu Whyte. Where is she staying? Tell me or I'll shoot the kid. And then you."

Moira's face froze. But Evolet had already made up his mind, and suddenly his hand flew up and grabbed the gun. He yanked it out of the attacker's hand in one quick, powerful twist, making the masked man himself the new target.

Evolet grinned. "I can ask you politely to leave, or I can just tell you to get lost before I—"

Much to the teenager's relief, the suggestion was all the masked stranger needed to turn and run. He soon disappeared into the blackness. Evolet straightened himself, dropping the gun onto the pavement outside the car, and touched his face. It had been stinging a few seconds before, but now as he touched it the pain was literally melting away, and the bleeding was stopping. Like every time he got hurt.

Moira was already collapsing back into her seat, breathing quickly as she pulled out her phone to call the cops. "Oh, Evolet," she breathed before she did, perhaps as a matter of habit, perhaps not. "What would I ever do without you?"

"Don't worry, I'll always b—" Evolet began automatically—but then he broke off.

He realized he might not always be there for her, if he was going to live with his parents—

No, he decided. He'd stay with Aunt Moira. For now, at least.

ten

Despite the fact that he didn't fall asleep until 3 AM—he was too busy thinking everything over repeatedly and getting up in the middle of the night for a snack—Evolet was by no means prepared to face Kai Lenon the next day at school.

The bully had been thoroughly humiliated the day before, and was out to get Evolet back—perhaps by getting him in trouble with the principal. Evolet, in turn, had forgotten all about their fallout.

So it came as something of a shock the next morning when the Whyte boy lingered outside the school building a few minutes before the bell to see if he could glimpse his sisters, that Kai approached him. The rude boy's gang openly backed him, waiting for Evolet to deign to pay him attention—an event which didn't happen.

Finally, as he only had a couple of minutes before classes would begin and they'd have to hurry inside, Kai gave up his patient waiting and addressed Evolet, who was actually a year younger.

"Hey, purple boy," he began, smirking. He was gratified, and somewhat surprised, to see Evolet visibly jump and look around wildly for a moment.

"Oh, it's you," the fourteen-year-old noted, somewhat relieved. "What do you want, Kai?"

"I wanna rematch," Kai told him imprudently. "One without cheating."

"I wasn't cheating," Evolet told him flatly, now remembering their match the day before. "Let me tell you, man, it's much easier to run on the ground than jump rooftops, see? I beat you fair and square. So what's your problem?"

"You're a creep." Kai ignored the question, intent on goading him into action. Kai was thicker in width, and felt he was stronger, and also felt he had a chance to beat him in a fight. Plus, a fight would get Evolet into trouble with the principal.

"Am I really?" Evolet asked vaguely, glancing over towards the middle school building again. He realized the twins had probably already been dropped off; at this point they were running late if they weren't at school yet. And so was he.

He started walking towards the entrance, reluctant to continue the conversation with Kai. He got past the door and into the lobby, and he had started heading for his locker when Kai's voice interrupted his thoughts.

"Yeah," Kai insisted. "All purple people are creeps. Like the Violet Army in the Purple Blitzkrieg—"

He stopped. Evolet had frozen, and was standing still directly in front of him.

Too still.

"What?" Kai demanded. And when Evolet didn't make to answer, he laughed triumphantly. "Oh! I bet you're actually in the Violet Army! Man, that's—"

He was shocked the next instant when Evolet spun around and grabbed him by the collar. "Take that back. Now."

There was an anger glowing in his purple eyes that Kai hadn't seen before, and he was momentarily taken aback. "Hey, man—"

"I said take it back," Evolet repeated intensely, and when Kai didn't answer right away, Evolet shook him slightly.

"What, it's the truth?" Kai grinned, recovering himself somewhat. "Oh boy, oh boy, that is creepy, bro—"

Evolet shoved him away with a force that made Kai suddenly reconsider fighting him. He stumbled backwards but didn't fall over. "Hey, you don't have to get violent!"

"Take it back, now," Evolet told him, stepping closer.

Kai backed up. "I don't take things back," he assured the younger boy stiffly, inwardly starting to feel somewhat uncomfortable.

He started to try to edge around to get to the hallway or outside, but Evolet efficiently blocked his escape in either direction.

"You do now," the younger boy gritted out. "I said take it back!"

"I won't—Mr. Rico!" Kai called out to their teacher as he was crossing the lobby to get to the classroom. The man turned around and saw the two for the first time.

"What are you doing, boys?" he demanded of them. "You're going to be late."

"We're just—" Evolet began, but Kai cut him off. "Evolet is trying to beat me up, Mr. Rico!"

"What?" the irritated teacher questioned, looking at them both and noticing Kai's messy collar. "Evolet?"

"Mr. Rico, I—" Evolet started again, flushing a violent red.

"Were you fighting?" Luis Rico continued as the truth dawned on him suddenly.

"N—no, not quite," Kai stammered, suddenly realizing that fighting might get him an unscheduled visit to the principal's office as well.

"Good." Luis shrugged dismissively. "Kai, I don't know why you aren't looking neat, but get to the bathroom and straighten your collar. If you're more than a minute late for class, I'll issue you demerits. Evolet, come here for a second. I want to talk to you."

Ignoring the older boy's spiteful glare as Kai hurried away, Evolet stepped over to their history teacher, breathing a sigh of relief. It would've been a real disgrace to be sent to the principal's office on the third day of high school—especially as Evolet had never been there a day in his life.

"Evolet." Luis turned to him. "I wasn't expecting to see you at school today."

Evolet blinked. "Oh," he said simply.

"This year, we're working backwards on the history timeline," Luis continued. "I thought your aunt would take you out of class today. But—"

"You mean we're going over the Purple Blitzkrieg?" Evolet asked quietly. "Because I know now."

"Oh, you do?" Luis's eyebrows shot up. Evolet nodded. "Okay, then," the teacher went on. "We're going to be watching a documentary, too. You can have a study hall if you want, seeing as—"

Evolet shook his head. "I want to attend the class. And please just ignore that I'm there. I want to know what happened. I—is that okay?"

Luis shrugged. "Alright. But if you need to leave, that's fine."

"I won't," Evolet assured him, making up his mind that he would watch the documentary and attend the lecture to the fullest. This was his family history, and he would have to know it even better than his classmates.

"Okay, you can head to class then," his teacher told him. Evolet turned to go, but Luis remembered something. "Oh, yes. Evolet?"

"Yes, sir?" Evolet paused, and turned around again to face his teacher.

"Were you fighting with Kai Lenon?" Luis asked him.

Evolet hesitated an instant before nodding as he stared at his shoes. "I'm sorry. I got mad."

"Evolet, you're a model student," Luis reminded him. "This is the first time." The boy nodded silently as he listened. "I'm not going to send you to the principal or give you detention, so long as it doesn't happen again."

"It won't," Evolet assured his teacher hastily. He looked up, hopefully.

"Good. But I have to call your aunt," Luis added.

Evolet's face fell. Moira was going to be so disappointed. "You do?"

"Yes, but don't worry. You'll be okay," Luis told him. "Now we'd better head to class or we'll be late."

"Thanks, Mr. Rico," Evolet told his teacher gratefully, running ahead down the hall to the door of the history classroom. Mr. Rico smiled as he watched the boy go.

eleven

"Citizens of Annapolis. This day marks the beginning of the Violet Empire. Annapolis is the first city to be incorporated into the Empire. Congratulations. My name is Trinity Ryder, and I am now your ruler. I want to warn you that any type of resistance will not be tolerated. None of it has a chance, as probably most of you know already. This invasion is not new; it began a week ago, and now it is finished, here in Annapolis... I will be watching you. My army is superhuman; you have no chance. I strongly advise you to behave. Or you won't find out how this ends."

Evolet wondered if the shooting he was seeing was real. He seriously doubted anyone would really have video footage of this. But he knew the voice was real, simply because he recognized the voice. He had a good ear for distinguishing that sort of thing, and he knew that this voice belonged to his mother.

She was definitely younger, he noted as he scrutinized the brief video clips of her speaking which were interspersed with "clips" of the massacres. Maybe twenty?

Then the speech ended, and the narrator's voice took over: a hard, deep man's voice that was obviously struggling to maintain an interesting, non-monotone pitch. Evolet would normally have struggled to repress a grin, but he was too absorbed in the line of gravestones. This was one war in which all the casualties had been identifiable, and they had been buried in new graveyards in their home cities. Evolet himself had been to the one in Annapolis, with Moira.

"Eighteen years ago, the greatest emergency in American history took place," the narrator began. The documentary had been made a year ago, Evolet calculated. "It also happens to be the greatest world crisis up to this point, and the one which we know the most about. Never before had enemies struck this close to home. And never will they again."

He's confident, Evolet thought grimly, knowing the saying "Only the dead have seen the end of war."

"This crisis is the Purple Blitzkrieg. It began at exactly 4:00 PM, December 1, 2024."

Evolet saw some of his classmates scribbling notes; Mr. Rico had told them they'd take a quiz on the documentary after it was finished. He smiled slightly, knowing everything he was seeing would be burned into his memory.

"It began in Annapolis, Maryland, as Violet Arnnu so kindly told us." Evolet caught his breath. "This Violet Arnnu—" There was a picture of Violet in battle gear, smiling— "—was the commander of the Violet Army. She called herself Trinity Ryder. The co-leader was her father, Lyndon Arnnu. We have been told that he was the main perpetrator of the Purple Blitzkrieg Massacres."

The picture of Violet dissolved into one of Lyndon. He wasn't smiling like Violet; he was sitting in what was obviously a prison cell, staring dismally at the floor.

Evolet swallowed hard, getting his first look at his grandfather. Suddenly he wondered if Lyndon was dead. Probably.

"Arnnu Senior had been working in secret for years, developing the first-ever superhuman serum. It took him four tries—the funding for which was stolen from Annapolis banks—and the fourth was successful: the T4."

Now the imaging was of some purple liquid, for a moment. Evolet stared, feeling somewhat uncomfortable as he realized that this was supposedly the injection that amplified his strength.

"Lyndon and his scientists also developed specialized combat suits, using a new material and a new element—Myelin—to absorb the shock from bullets. This semi-liquid substance is also highly dangerous, and the only existing sample of it is in freezer biocontainment in Texas.

"When they were ready, they published their discoveries by an abrupt invasion of Annapolis. But this invasion was silent and deadly. For a week, their submissive drug was in the public water sources of Annapolis. Using this tactic, the Violet Army took control on December 1, 2024."

Shots of the massacres were shown again: Navy classes interrupted with purple-clad soldiers and their lethal guns; police officers, gunned down.

Evolet was tense. This was a documentary shown only to high school students, and he could see why.

"The Violet Army spread their conquests like lightning. An attack from the United States followed, but was driven off."

His mom was back, leading a strike team through the streets of Annapolis, hunting U.S. paratroopers. Evolet froze when he noticed her pointing out a runner to a soldier who mostly just followed behind. He stared hard at the soldier, who then shot, making a perfect hit.

And then the soldier pushed his visor up, and for a brief second Evolet could see his face.

His mouth dropped open in shock.

It was definitely Conner, but there was also something very definitely wrong with his face and blank expression.

Evolet decided it must be the drug.

"And it is about here that the true heroes of the Purple Blitzkrieg entered the conflict," the narrator went on, and suddenly a picture of Moira's face filled the screen. She was sixteen in the picture, Evolet decided, quickly counting the years.

Moira's picture zoomed out to reveal her, Giulia Pervitto, and Niamh French walking towards a ground-level camera. Above them, Evolet noticed black specks in the sky and wondered briefly what they were.

"Moira Whyte," the narrator announced, and a few of the kids glanced at Evolet in surprise. "She very likely saved the entire United States by refusing to believe that her twin brother, Conner Whyte, was dead. She was correct: Conner Whyte had been abducted, injected, and drugged by the Violet Army. He was actually the first of their supersoldiers."

They had a picture of him, strapped to a chair, the same vacant expression on his face.

Evolet tipped his chair back absently and stared at his father's face nineteen years before.

"Moira Whyte wouldn't believe that he was dead, even when the police found and dealt with whom they believed to be the murderer. Instead of giving up, she became a hacker, and finally succeeded in gaining access to Encephalon files—unfortunately, only on the day of the attack. She and her friends, Nina Marwick, John Marwick, Clotilde Marwick, and Lucinda Montoya formed a secret group to get the Violet Army's clandestine files to the United States government. Their plan failed, but in the meantime, other forces were at work."

The screen switched from an overview of the Encephalon homepage to a picture of Joyce Liszt. She, everyone knew. She was the famous superhuman Marine paratrooper—the one whom Evolet had always considered himself lucky to be able to call "Aunt Joyce." Of course, there wasn't a blood relationship—as far as he knew.

But then it dawned on him that he had seen Aunt Giulia and Aunt Niamh in the footage, too. Were all his "close relatives" he'd grown up around, close only because of the Purple Blitzkrieg?

"Joyce Liszt, U.S. Marine paratrooper," the speaker announced needlessly. Someone in the back of the classroom tittered. "And her friend Erin French, were the only two American paratroopers to succeed in getting behind the lines. They joined forces with Darek Lasek and Niamh French. Niamh— Erin's cousin—was a former Annapolis police officer who left the force to take a teaching job. Darek Lasek was also a veteran police officer, who'd been honorably discharged because of an injury, which coincidentally happened during the Whyte case."

Evolet smiled at the picture of his Uncle Darek smiling frankly. He really liked Darek, the only "uncle" he knew. Darek had taught him the bit of shooting and combat tips he knew—Moira hated that sort of stuff, and besides Darek was a professional.

"During the first day of the Blitzkrieg, Moira realized that her brother was in the Violet Army. Events followed so quickly that during the next morning, we have been told that she had a chance to shoot at the Violet Army leader—

Violet Arnnu—but, unluckily for her, the attempt failed, as Arnnu's trusty bodyguard Conner Whyte was there, and shot at his sister without realizing it."

Evolet gasped in horror, as did many of the girls—before realizing that Luis Rico was looking directly at him, hard. He shut his mouth with a snap and riveted his attention on the screen. He would not react.

"Fortunately for him and for the American cause, his sister survived—and Conner Whyte regained his memories, which the Violet Army scientists had erased. Several days followed, in which he was kept a strict prisoner. Rumor has it that Lyndon wanted to eliminate him and be done with it, but that Violet insisted on keeping him alive until he would join them."

There was a short video of Conner screaming his defiance, and, try as he would not to, Evolet had to cringe. And his blood ran cold when the clip was followed by an image of Violet, delivering her ultimatum.

He couldn't believe that this was how his parents had really met. This was insanely horrifying. He wondered if Kai had seen this documentary before, and that was why he'd called him a creep.

But this was past just purple-creepiness. This was terrifying.

"Liszt, Lasek, and the two Frenches discovered his prison, as well as Nina Marwick's—who had been captured by the Violet Army—and broke in to rescue them, in hopes that the two teenagers could give them some information. The operation was successful, and the six of them teamed up with Moira, John, and Clotilde, who had meanwhile joined Giulia Pervitto—formerly a waitress in an Italian restaurant. It was these ten that prepared for the final attack on Encephalon."

For the next ten minutes, Evolet and his classmates watched breathlessly as the final battle and battles played out on the screen. The narrator cut out completely, leaving the Encephalon security cameras and microphones to speak for themselves. And they did. The fourteen-year-old became white-faced and tight-lipped as the fighting went on, with a low, quiet background music that somehow added an aura of unreality to the whole thing.

Evolet bit his lip as the realization sunk in that this wasn't a movie. This was real, and it was his parents.

Still, he was somewhat disturbed when things calmed down after the ten were captured. They were talking quietly at the opposite end of the room from the camera before Violet and a few others came in, from an angle below the camera view.

Then a leader, Hilton Maughan, ordered a soldier named Louis Staunton to finish them all—and Violet intervened. The creepy part was how the camera zoomed in at the side of her face, and those watching could see the cold look in her eyes as she gave her instructions.

There was rapid fire of speaking between Violet and Conner, and another fight broke out. The lights cut and there were just sounds: shouts, screams, and shots. The music got louder, almost drowning out the sounds of battle. But then a single voice yelled above the others, and the music cut, leaving just the voice.

"STOP! We can't win. You guys can keep fighting if you want. But I'm joining Trooper."

He knew it was Violet's voice. But he froze even as it dawned on him.

Was *that* why she had teamed up with Conner? What!

The narrator took over now, finishing the events briefly. Anger kindled in Evolet's eyes as he heard the man very emphatically portray his mother as a coward who'd joined the U.S. simply because she was losing. Then the narrator went on to explain how Violet Arnnu escaped justice—by bribing her coworkers to keep silent about her, coworkers that were later executed by order of the Supreme Court.

The speaker finished by pointing out dryly how she'd ignored the fact that her father had been arrested and condemned and instead had started a new life of her own, a national hero—till the American people had finally realized she had no place among them.

The documentary finished with photos of the new White House—the motion to call it the Whyte House in honor of the popular heroes of the day had been promptly and emphatically turned down by Senator Adrien Whyte and his embarrassed family.

Evolet smiled at one picture that had his late grandparents in it. He could still remember them, even though they'd passed away when he was much younger. And he and his aunt Moira often took trips to visit their graves and pray for them.

The happy music evaporated into the *Star Spangled Banner,* with credits showing. Their teacher turned it off hurriedly.

"Okay, everyone," he spoke up as his students stretched and yawned—excluding Evolet. "We're gonna take a quiz now. Evolet, can you pass 'em out?"

"Yes sir," Evolet replied automatically, standing up. He hurried over to the teacher's desk, grabbed the stack of papers, and marched around the classroom, making sure everyone got a copy.

Sitting down at his own desk, he stared at the paper, running his hands through his hair nervously.

"You may all begin," came Mr. Rico's command, though sharp-eared Evolet could hear that some students were already starting."You have ten minutes. Don't forget to check it over—it's an easy hundred, unless you slept through the whole thing."

Evolet nodded absently, picking up his pencil and beginning to fill in the blanks, circling multiple-choice letters, etc. He was soon nearly finished, but the second-to-the-last question made him stop and stare.

Why did Violet Arnnu join the American side?

A: She wanted to trick them so she could win more easily.

B: She knew she was losing, so she wanted to save face.

C: She didn't join the American side.

D: She was sick of fighting and really believed in the American cause.

Evolet ran his hands through his hair again. Twice. He let out a soft whistle of deliberation.

According to the documentary, the answer was *B*, he knew. But he also knew he didn't want to believe *B* could be true. He wanted to say *D*. But he wasn't even sure if *D* was correct, and he *was* sure that if he chose it he'd be marked wrong.

A keen wave of agonized disappointment flowed through him suddenly as he remembered Violet's creepy smile in a lot of the pictures and videoing. The one that had made him shudder.

Could *D* be true?

Wasn't it better to just trust to the documentary?

But he didn't want to. He didn't want to put down *B*, because in his serious frame of mind he felt like it would be a betrayal.

A betrayal of his mother, if she really wasn't that bad—and if she was, which he sincerely hoped she wasn't, then a betrayal of his old dreams of a wonderful, kind, caring mother.

Nobody's perfect, he reminded himself.

But he *wanted* his mother to be perfect. And with sudden resolve he picked up his pencil and circled *D.*

He sat back, tipping his chair slightly. There. It was done. He wasn't going to change it. Quickly, he marked the answer to the last question. The quiz was finished.

He was going to regret that later, he knew, when he got the test back with a 90%. That would be low for him. Ordinarily, Evolet had no trouble at all staying at the top of his class. But he knew he would regret the grade much less than he would have regretted admitting to himself that his mother might be a bad guy after all.

She still could be, a voice whispered, deep down inside him. Evolet glared at his desk.

"She isn't," he whispered to himself. "She can't be."

But try as he would, he couldn't make the doubt go away.

twelve

Kai had not been ignoring Evolet's reactions to the documentary. In fact, he had been paying more attention to his classmate than to the video, as Mr. Rico might have sensed when he gave him a 50% later that evening. Kai was definitely eager to bombard Evolet with what he *had* learned.

"Purple boy!" he shouted as their teacher left the room. "Whaddya think of your girly eyes now?"

Evolet started, then glanced over at him. A flash of annoyance crossed his face. "What's your problem, Kai?" he asked the older boy for the third time in two days.

"You're in the Violet Army." Kai went on, ignoring the question. "Why're you here at our school?"

"The war ended twenty years ago, silly," Evolet told him absently. His mind was still racing.

"Aww, leave him alone, Kai," another kid broke in from behind Evolet's desk. "It could be just a coincidence."

Evolet turned around slightly to see a boy he hadn't met before. The boy smiled slightly, and Evolet managed to smile back.

"It is just a coincidence, right?" the boy added timidly.

Evolet half-shrugged. He didn't feel much like talking. Turning his attention back to his desk, he played with his hair and then started scribbling on a piece of paper. He wasn't a very good artist, but he had a dim feeling he was trying to sketch Jasmine's face.

But all around him he could hear his classmates discussing the documentary, and he felt his cheeks burning. He spoke very little for the rest of the morning. In fact he was still so quiet after school that he didn't say much, even when he met Jasmine and a new friend named Livia Parson. He didn't talk much even when Moira showed up in a rental car and explained— needlessly—that her own was in for repairs.

Moira tried to get him into a flowing conversation, but nothing worked until she noted, "Mr. Rico called me today. Your teacher."

"Oh." Evolet jumped, shaking himself out of his apathy. He glanced at his aunt anxiously.

Moira repressed a smile and made her face stern. "He said he caught you fighting with another student today?"

"Oh." Evolet swallowed nervously and looked away. "Yeah. That."

"What was that all about?" Moira went on severely.

Evolet stared down at his shoes. "I'm sorry. I got mad—at—at him. I won't do it again," he promised quickly.

"There is a reason I have always told you not to fight with anyone, you know," Moira reprimanded him.

"I know," Evolet whispered. "It won't happen again," he assured her. "I'll control myself. Even if he is a—" He broke off.

"Good." Moira allowed herself a smile. "And he also told me your class was watching a documentary on the Purple Blitzkrieg. How'd that go?"

"Okay, I guess," Evolet answered hesitantly. He desperately wanted—had been wanting—to ask his aunt about his mother.

But he was afraid to. What if she just told him enough that he wouldn't feel bad?

He didn't want to know the truth. If it was the truth. So he didn't ask.

"That's great," Moira commented, watching her nephew curiously out of the corner of her eye. She knew he'd been fretting; his hair was more neatly "brushed" than it had been in forever. He nodded absently.

"Your siblings and parents are coming over," she told him suddenly.

He snapped out of his reverie again. "They are?" he asked, sounding surprised.

Moira nodded. "In fact they're coming to stay for a while, till your parents find a house. That's why I had you clean your room—Charles is going to be staying with you."

"Ooo," Evolet muttered, not feeling too excited as he remembered his nine-year-old little brother's seemingly constant blustering and competitiveness. "What about the others?" he asked interestedly a few seconds later.

"The twins'll be in my room," Moira explained, "and Conner and Violet will get your grandparents' room. It might be somewhat snug, but we'll all fit," she laughed.

Evolet smiled slightly. "Of course we will."

"Conner wanted me to ask if you wanted to go with them when they move, or if you want to stay with me," Moira continued.

She didn't look at her nephew. Secretly she felt that if she were to lose Evolet—she didn't know.

"Oh." Evolet sat back in the passenger seat, a slight smile on his face. "I'm gonna stay with you, I think," he replied quickly.

Moira glanced at him in surprise until she realized she was about to crash. She swerved her attention back to the road, and the car jolted away from the sidewalk.

"You do?" she asked, trying not to sound as relieved as she was.

He nodded emphatically. "I can still visit them, right?"

"Well of course!" Moira exclaimed. "But I was thinking you'd want—"

"Are you kidding me?" Evolet asked her incredulously. "What if something happened...like last night?"

"True," Moira admitted. She sighed. "The police didn't find any finger-prints on the gun, by the way. Except your own."

"How'd they even get my fingerprints?" Evolet demanded in a slightly injured tone of voice.

Moira shrugged. "I dunno. Maybe they could tell from the size that they were a kid's fingerprints."

Evolet brushed his hand across his face, pausing at the place he'd been cut the night before. It didn't hurt in the least now.

"Well, I guess that means he was wearing gloves. But why'd he ask about Mom?" The teenager frowned.

Moira frowned as well. "That's what I want to know, too," she admitted. She sighed. "Anyway. Leave it to the police. Have you got any homework?"

"Homework?" Evolet echoed, taken aback by the sudden change of subject. "Not really. I finished most of it already."

"Then let's go to the park," Moira decided suddenly, making a quick turn, away from their house and in the direction of an Annapolis park. "It's someone's birthday, I heard, and all the ninth-grade kids and their families got invited."

"Why didn't you tell me?" Evolet asked half-sulkily, though he was grinning his head off.

Moira shrugged. "I dunno. I didn't think you'd want to go, I guess. But if you'll grab my phone out of my bag, and dial Conner, I bet you can invite your siblings." She grinned as Evolet dove for the device.

thirteen

Fifteen minutes later found Evolet, Jasmine, and Jasmine's friend Livia Parson talking together in a corner of the park, sitting on some rocks. Jasmine was glad to see her older brother looking more like he had the other night, and she had been absolutely overjoyed to find Livia at the party as well.

Evolet and Livia had already been introduced, but Jasmine excitedly introduced them again, and the three had grabbed hotdogs and headed for a quieter place. The three of them—Jasmine refused to let either Evolet or Livia disappear—dangled their legs from a rock that was like a mini clifftop: Livia on one side of Jasmine, and Evolet on the other.

Jasmine was quick to hook the others in a conversation about school. She and Livia did most of the talking, with Evolet interjecting some comments randomly whenever he felt like it.

"School is so much fun," the superhuman twelve-year-old was telling the other two. She took a small bite of hotdog and swallowed it hastily before she continued. "The teachers are nicer than Mom and Dad. And the homework is super easy!"

"You've only been to school three days now," Livia put in somewhat disparagingly. "What would you know about it?" She was a social type, tall—though not as tall as Jasmine or Evolet—with short, curly golden hair. Despite her temperament, she was a target for some of her not-so-friendly classmates, though Jasmine had ended that on the first day.

"Evolet, isn't school fun?" Jasmine demanded of her older brother.

He shrugged. "I dunno, is it?"

"Oh, you—" Jasmine did her best to glare ferociously, which might have worked if she hadn't been naturally nice and amiable, with an irrepressible smile.

Evolet grinned. She was so funny.

Or maybe he just thought that because he was her older brother.

"Just wait till the homework gets harder," Livia told Jasmine morbidly. "Because it will, you'll see. Evolet could tell you that."

Jasmine shrugged, tossing her brown hair. "I don't care," she insisted. "I like it anyway."

"Did you hear what happened last night?" Evolet asked, forgetting that Livia was there. He stretched luxuriously, thoroughly bored of the topic of school. There were more interesting things in life, after all.

"No?" Jasmine sounded surprised. "What happened last night?"

"Well, if you don't know, maybe I shouldn't tell you," Evolet reasoned, closing his eyes.

"Tell me or I will knock you off the rock," Jasmine threatened immediately, extremely curious. Livia giggled.

Evolet opened one eye, and his eyebrows shot up. "Mhmm. Sure."

"I will," Jasmine assured him seriously.

"Fine then." Evolet shrugged. "Someone shot Aunt Moira's car tires."

"What!" Jasmine gasped. Livia sat up straighter and stared frankly at the high schooler.

"Yeah," Evolet added, enjoying the attention. "And they asked about—" He suddenly glanced at Livia, realizing she was still there. "...Mom," he finished lamely.

"They asked about Mom?" Jasmine questioned, her face suddenly turning serious. Livia was watching both the siblings curiously.

Evolet nodded. "Mhmm. But I got rid of whoever it was."

"Does Mom know?" Jasmine whispered.

Her older brother shrugged. "I dunno. I'm willing to assume Aunt Moira told our parents."

"What about you guys' mom?" Livia asked curiously.

"Oh, nothing," Jasmine shrugged it off. Evolet glanced at her, somewhat relieved to see that she wasn't blabbing out their whole family history.

"How'd you 'get rid of whoever it was'?" Livia burst out, but then she answered her own question. "Hey, you're like Jaz and Ali?"

"I guess," Evolet admitted, and laughed shortly.

"That's so cool," Livia breathed.

"He's even cooler than we are," Jasmine added in her good-natured way. "He likes to climb." Evolet felt his cheeks turning red.

"I can see that," Livia grinned pointedly.

"Imma learn to climb just as good," Jasmine added, unhampered in the least. "I should teach you, too."

Livia looked dubious. "Yeah, right. Like I could learn to be...athletic like you are?"

"Oh, sure you can," Jasmine grinned at her best friend of three days. "Someday. It'll be fun!"

Livia's eyes sparkled. "I'm sure it will be," she agreed dreamily. Evolet got the impression that perhaps Livia Parson wasn't as athletic as normal kids. Maybe that was why she and Jasmine had become quick besties.

"Hey, Dad used to be real thin," Jasmine pointed out excitedly. "He said he was really weak too. But he's very strong now. So—"

"Jaz," Evolet interrupted warningly, and she stopped abruptly.

"So you think there's hope for me?" Livia demanded.

Evolet closed his eyes, remembering the purple liquid from the documentary. He tensed.

"Maybe."

He grinned as Jasmine went obliviously onto other conversation topics. Finishing his hotdog, he stared at the sky and watched the sun dip below the horizon. Suddenly he blinked, realizing Jasmine had said his name.

"Evolet," she repeated, sounding a bit cross. "Aunt Moira's calling you."

"Oh," he nodded quickly, jumping up. "See you, Jaz. See you, Livia."

"See ya!" The two best friends waved after him as he leapt down from the rocks like a mountain goat and shot off to find his aunt.

"He's so fast," Livia muttered, watching him.

"I know, right?" Jasmine grinned.

fourteen

The days, weeks, and months that followed flew by for Evolet, until it was Thanksgiving Vacation: two weeks off from schoolwork.

He was sitting on his bed Wednesday afternoon, reading absently as he listened to the girls talking in the kitchen. His mother, Aunt Moira, Jasmine, and Alison were in there, cooking food for the next day. They'd be spending Thanksgiving at Moira's house and spending the night there as well. Evolet was sharing his room again.

Evolet smiled to himself. He'd gotten to know his siblings pretty well at this point: friendly Jasmine, scornful Alison, and annoying Charles. Then his parents, too. They were both pretty quiet—but...*real*.

He wondered where his dad was as he heard Charles's young, sharp voice pipe up in protest at his dismissal from the kitchen. The older brother's unvoiced question was answered a moment later as someone knocked on his door.

"Yeah?" Evolet asked, looking up from his book.

"Can I come in?" Conner asked, his voice coming through the door slightly muffled.

"Oh, sure." Evolet grinned, and sat up straighter as his father pushed the door open and stepped in.

"Hey, son," Conner greeted him, smiling. "Wanna go for a walk? It's stopped raining."

"It has?" Evolet realized, glancing out the window. He dropped his book on his bed and slid down to the floor, launching himself towards his shoes, which were by the door. Conner was already dressed for walking, and he waited patiently for the fourteen-year-old to finish tying his shoes.

"You mean a run, not a walk, right?" Evolet smirked as he finished and stood up, stretching.

"Hmm, I guess we'll see," Conner returned casually.

Evolet grabbed his coat, shrugging it on and then zipping it up. "Where are we going?"

Ten seconds later found the two of them running through the slushy streets of Annapolis, Conner just slightly ahead with Evolet close on his heels. Not many people were driving their cars on the wet afternoon before Thanksgiving, and even fewer were out walking, so the father and son were relatively alone.

Finally Conner ended the headlong dash by climbing to the top of a high, grid-patterned truss of a bridge. Evolet followed him up doggedly, eventually making it to the top girder. He sat down next to his father, a hundred feet or so above the roadway and the water beneath it. He was panting.

"I'll never be as fast as you," he complained once he had enough breath to speak.

Conner grinned encouragingly. "You're good. You're *really* good. At your age, I—"

"I know," Evolet interrupted him, a smile breaking out on his face. "At my age you couldn't do anything I can. You've told me so many times."

"That's right," Conner had to admit. He smiled proudly.

"So how's it going with Moira?" he asked the teenager a few seconds later.

Evolet shrugged. "Like normal, I guess."

"How's school?" his father went on. "Are you getting your first quarter report soon?"

"Yeah, we should get them by the end of Thanksgiving break," Evolet nodded, having caught his breath somewhat.

"Your grades better be good," Conner warned him mock-severely.

Evolet giggled. "They are," he assured his father. "You'll see."

"Your birthday is coming up, isn't it," Conner mused thoughtfully.

The almost fifteen-year-old flushed. "Yeah. Next Tuesday. Good thing it's during Thanksgiving break," he added, laughing a bit.

"Is your party gonna be at Moira's, or at our house?" Conner kept up the rapid fire of questions.

Evolet shrugged. "I dunno. I don't care, really."

"Yeah, you're at our house a lot." Conner nodded. "Good thing, too," he added as an afterthought, "or we'd really miss you."

Evolet smiled slightly. "I'd miss you, too."

"Does Livia Parson still hang out with you and Jaz?" Conner wanted to know. "I haven't heard much about her lately, though usually she's all Jaz can talk about after school."

The boy shrugged. "I dunno. She's more of Jaz's friend than mine, of course," he pointed out. "I think Jaz said she's sick."

"Oh," Conner said simply.

Evolet nodded, being a kid who'd never spent a day in his life being sick.

"Well, I hope she gets better soon," Conner admitted. "From what I can tell, she's the only friend Jaz has really been able to make."

"Yeah," Evolet nodded.

"Have you got any friends at school?" Conner wanted to know. "Moira told me your old best friend moved away."

Evolet shrugged, thinking of Kai. He scowled. "I dunno."

Conner laughed.

"You should just talk to people," he told Evolet. "There's got to be someone in your class who—"

"They don't want to talk to me," Evolet broke in. "One of the kids keeps saying I'm in the...the Violet Army," he finished awkwardly.

Conner glanced at his eldest in surprise. "They know?"

"No." Evolet shook his head. "But I think they're afraid of me."

"Well, at least you have a little brother now to keep you company," Conner pointed out, smiling.

Evolet laughed.

"Does *anyone* at school know?" Conner went on, sobering up somewhat.

Evolet shook his head. "No, not unless Jaz told Livia."

"Well, let's keep it that way," Conner told him seriously. "Because the threats haven't stopped."

The teenager tensed. "They haven't? But Aunt Moira hasn't been talking about them."

Almost immediately after Conner, Violet, and the family had returned to the United States, Aunt Moira—and Conner and Violet—had started getting threats. Evolet only knew about them because he'd been given one once, by a stranger who'd stopped him on the street, stared at his face, pressed a paper into his hand, and darted away.

By the time Evolet had read the note—*Where is Violet?*—the man had disappeared into the crowd. Conner and Moira had told him not to tell any of his siblings about it, and so he hadn't.

"No, they haven't stopped. And don't tell your siblings," Conner added quickly. "I'm only telling you because you're the oldest."

"I won't tell them," Evolet assured him eagerly. "What are the people after?"

Conner shook his head. "We don't know yet. And the police are clueless."

Evolet sighed. "Why would anyone threaten us? And why about Mom?"

A sad look came over his father's face. "I wish I knew. But some people don't like your Mom—or us," he added quickly.

It was on the tip of Evolet's tongue to ask about the documentary, but he didn't. "But why?" he asked again slowly. "Is that why Mom looks so worried all the time now?" he continued, remembering how he hadn't seen his mother smile in weeks.

"I only wish I knew," Conner repeated softly. He frowned. "Promise me, whatever happens, you'll take care of Aunt Moira. And your siblings."

"But—" Evolet began.

"The threats aren't exactly friendly," Conner interjected. "And since they're mostly about me and your mother..."

"No one could hurt you two," Evolet laughed incredulously.

"So far, we don't even know who they are," Conner pointed out seriously.

Evolet had to nod. "Okay then. But nothing will happen," he added, more to himself than to his father. "If we all stick together, we'll be fine." He watched his feet dangling above the distant road.

"Hopefully," Conner agreed. "If we stick together."

fifteen

"Just because you're older and stronger doesn't mean you can be nasty, Ali."

A snicker. "And you're the nice one, eh?"

Evolet sighed, standing up from the steps as he heard his twin sisters' voices mingling in angry, loud conversation as they rounded the corner of the high school building. He glanced over at them.

They were wearing their matching uniforms and purple sweaters as usual, and this time both were glaring furiously. But he could still tell them apart: Jasmine was the one walking with Livia, and Alison was the one with her long bangs half-covering her eyes. Jasmine had trimmed her bangs some days ago. It hadn't yet snowed in Annapolis, though it was early December, a week or so after Thanksgiving and Evolet's birthday.

Watching his younger sisters, Evolet could guess what this new argument was about. Probably Alison and her small group of friends—he didn't quite want to think of them as bullies, but from what he'd heard that's what they were—had been bothering Livia again, and Jasmine had stepped in to the rescue as usual. The twins were infuriated at each other, and Livia looked somewhat worried.

"It's your fault if you don't wanna be nice," Jasmine returned heatedly. "You could at least—"

"You don't even seem to realize that you're as strong as you are! You shouldn't be afraid to be yourself!" Alison countered scornfully.

"I'm not!" Jasmine gritted. "You're the one thinking you have to be mean to look tough! But believe me, you're not!"

"I can beat you anytime," Alison hissed.

"'Cept you can't," Jasmine disagreed emphatically. "And if you don't leave Livia alone, I'll—"

"Don't," Livia broke in, her voice wavering. "Come on guys, just forget it. I'm fine, Jaz."

Jasmine ignored her friend. "Really, Ali, you have to stop it."

"Oh, and who's gonna make me?" Alison smirked. "*You?*"

"Yes," Jasmine responded emphatically. "I will."

"You couldn't," Alison argued confidently. "I'm stronger than you!"

"No you aren't!" Jasmine returned, her eyes flashing fiercely. "And Mom and Dad say you shouldn't use your strength to—"

"Hey, Ali, Jaz, stop arguing," Evolet broke in, walking over to the three. "What's up? You're making enough noise to pop a balloon."

"Jaz's being pathetic," Alison returned, just as Jasmine shouted, "Ali won't stop bullying people!"

The now fifteen-year-old sighed, running his hands through his hair and staring at the three, who stared back.

"Ali, why do you have to bother other people?" he asked finally, cautiously. He didn't want to get into this argument, himself.

Alison glared at her younger twin sister. "Why do you have to take her side!" she hissed at Evolet. "Just because she's your favorite doesn't mean she's better or stronger."

"Hey, this isn't about better or stronger, and ten minutes older doesn't make much of a difference there anyway," Evolet returned calmly. "I'm talking about *you*, not her. Why do you—"

"Because I'm stronger than they are," Alison explained passionately.

Evolet's eyebrows shot up. "Well, then, why don't you prove that some other way? Like race them or something?"

"Racing is boring." Alison's bottom lip curled in scorn.

"I'll race you," Jasmine told her older sister, glaring ferociously. "It won't be boring anymore when I win."

"But you won't!" Alison returned quickly, her eyes sparking fire.

Evolet held up a hand, and the two were momentarily silenced. "If you're gonna race, you better do it before Mom and Dad get here," he suggested.

"Oh yes." Alison smirked.

Jasmine grinned defiantly. "Where to?"

Within five seconds the two were off. Evolet sighed again, wishing they wouldn't be constantly arguing. He hated arguments, especially among siblings, but maybe that was because he hadn't had siblings for most of his life.

Livia shrugged as she watched them run, and then glanced over to where Moira was parking her car. "When'll they be back?" she wondered aloud.

"Oh, soon I guess," Evolet replied, pulling his backpack straps tighter and starting to head over to his aunt's car. "The bakery isn't that far away."

Livia's eyebrows went up, as she was somewhat doubtful of that, but she shrugged and remained silent. Evolet waved as he went to the car, and Livia waved back slightly. She watched for the twins, shielding her eyes from the sun with one hand.

Meanwhile Evolet was surprised to find that Charles was already in Moira's car. He was even more surprised when Moira told him to get the girls.

"Aren't Mom and Dad driving 'em home?" he asked, confused.

"Not today," Moira shook her head. "Where are they?"

"They're...racing," Evolet admitted. "They'll be back in a few minutes."

One of Moira's eyebrows arched. "Do they always race when their ride is waiting?"

"N—no." Evolet repressed a grin as he saw his aunt struggling with one of her own.

Moira shrugged hopelessly. "Well, hop in then."

Evolet took her literally, jerking the passenger door open and leaping onto the seat. Charles made faces from the middle seat, and Evolet returned the favor by grinning like an idiot at his younger brother, who burst into boyish giggles.

A few minutes later, the twins came into view, both panting hard and even with each other. They were still even when they got to where Livia was holding her hands out as an ending point. Even inside the car, Evolet could hear his twelve-year-old sisters literally screaming at each other.

He grimaced. A tie wasn't going to make anything better.

"I'm still stronger than you!"

"Obviously not! I would've beaten you if you hadn't—"

Moira opened her car window. "Ali! Jaz! It's time to go!"

The twins turned, seeing the vehicle for the first time. Alison started running over, but Jasmine lingered a few seconds to bid goodbye to her best friend. Evolet saw them grin at each other and high-five, and then Jasmine came running over to Moira's car, tumbling in after her sister.

"Aren't Mom and Dad picking us up?" Jasmine asked her aunt as she grabbed her seat belt and buckled it.

"They're busy," Charles answered before Moira could.

"That's right—we're going to your house first, so you three can pick up what you'll need for the weekend," Moira explained.

"What are they busy with?" Evolet wanted to know.

"They're gonna be gone for the whole weekend?" Alison demanded.

"Do Ali and I get to sleep in your room again?" Jasmine asked excitedly.

Moira glanced around the car to make sure they were ready to leave. "Evolet, Alison—buckle up. I don't know how long they'll be gone. Yes, Jaz, you do."

"You didn't answer my question," Evolet complained as he and Alison buckled their seat belts.

Moira smiled slightly. "That's because it's a secret."

"Aww, not another secret." The teenager frowned. "I hate secrets!"

"Oh, well." Moira shrugged as she took the car out of park mode and started it. "Too bad!"

sixteen

Some hours later, after supper at Moira's house, Jasmine knocked gently at the door of the boys' room. Evolet stepped out a few seconds later.

"Hey, what's up, Jaz?" he asked quietly, noting that she was dressed for running, a light jacket tied around her waist.

She smiled. "I was just wondering if you knew what's going on with Mom and Dad."

Evolet frowned slightly. "How would I know?"

Jasmine shrugged. "You've been thoughtful lately. Like Dad. Or is it just because you're growing up?" she teased.

Her older brother pulled a face. "Hey, I'm only fifteen," he protested.

"Mhmm," Jasmine nodded. "But seriously, don't you wonder what's going on, too?"

"I dunno," Evolet shrugged carefully. "I guess we'll find out eventually, right?"

"I guess—" Jasmine began.

Charles popped his head out of Evolet's bedroom door. "Whatcha talkin' 'bout?" he demanded curiously.

Jasmine hastily backed away, towards the front door. "Nothing—I'm going to go for a run!" she called to her brothers, dashing outside.

She stopped on the front porch, frowning as she glanced back at the door, obviously debating on whether or not she should go back in and keep talking to Evolet. She was just as obviously dealing with some conflicting thoughts, but finally she shrugged, and started jogging down the street.

Meanwhile, Conner and Violet were sitting in the car across the street, talking quietly.

"Looks like it's going to be quiet today," Violet remarked. She was watching a live feed of their home on her small laptop. "Quieter than I've seen it in my life. After we moved in, of course."

"Well, that makes sense," Conner nodded. "But whoever is threatening us has to strike eventually."

"Especially after telling us to watch the kids," Violet agreed. "Well, they're getting what they want."

"Maybe we should've gone back to Iceland after all," Conner admitted softly.

Violet nodded emphatically. "That's what I've been telling you for the past week or so!"

"But we have to face them sometime," Conner muttered, "and running away will get us nowhere. If they really want to take us out, they'll just follow us. And besides, if we went back to Iceland, we'd have to leave Evolet and Moira here."

"Couldn't we just bring Evolet?" Violet frowned. "Your sister will be fine."

"We don't know that," Conner shook his head. He sighed. "Evolet thinks we should all stick together."

Violet bit her lip, and closed her eyes. "We're safer away from here."

Conner glanced at her out of the corner of his eye, wondering for the hundredth time in the past month if there was something Violet knew and he didn't. It was on the tip of his tongue to ask her, but he'd already done so, and gotten nothing more than "I have only suspicions."

He sighed again, wishing for the millionth time that they could just live normal lives. But that was impossible in a family like theirs.

"Oh, there's Jaz," he realized a second later as Jasmine jogged past them obliviously. "What's she doing out? I told Moira not to let them out."

"Maybe Moira doesn't know," Violet pointed out dryly. "Should we follow Jaz? Or tell her to get back inside?"

"The kids shouldn't know that we're watching them," Conner shook his head. "I'm going to call Moira. Oh, heavens," he added as Jasmine suddenly picked up speed, "you'd better go follow her."

"Right," Violet agreed, zipping up her trademark purple jacket a few inches higher and popping her car door open, just as Conner dialed his twin's number.

Violet waited a few seconds before dashing after her youngest daughter discreetly, staying on the other side of the road. She could keep up with her easily, but didn't want to, knowing Jasmine would probably notice an obvious follower. So she stayed somewhat behind, meanwhile recounting to herself the events that had led up to this.

It had all started the night they came back to the United States. The threats had begun again immediately, starting with Moira's car being shot at. Evolet's effective means of ridding them of the stranger had evidently made the stranger more cautious, because from then on the threats had been mostly on paper—excluding a few narrow car crashes, some angry crowds, and various other attempts to injure the Whytes.

And now someone had called Conner, saying they were going to hurt the children. So Conner, Violet, and Moira had quickly come up with a plan, which involved Moira keeping the kids at her house and Conner and Violet watching the house. They would try to find out who was doing this. And they would put an end to it.

Except Jasmine wasn't in the house anymore. Violet sighed. Maybe Moira had forgotten to tell them to stay inside. But it didn't matter, because Moira would probably come running out any second now and yell for Jasmine. Then Violet could go back to waiting in the car—which was actually quite boring—

Violet did not miss the car that suddenly swung into Jasmine's path, coming to a screeching stop just as Jasmine slammed into the hood. The twelve-year-old stumbled back, slightly dazed.

The young mother increased her running speed to top capacity even before she saw the driver's door open and a darkly-dressed man dash out and over to the young girl.

Anyone else would have assumed that he was shocked at having run into the girl and was going to help her, but something in his tall height, dark brown hair, hard-set jaw, and flashing gray eyes froze Violet in horror.

Violet fairly swung herself up over a car that got in her way, and flew the remaining distance over to her daughter, but she arrived on the scene a few seconds too late.

Before Jasmine could recover, the man had shoved her into the back of the car. The vehicle fishtailed from side to side as its driver swerved around the corner at a hundred miles per hour, obviously trying to lose Violet.

The mother kept up for a few minutes but then had to give up. She nearly collapsed on the side of the road, watching the car as it disappeared.

She fished her phone out of her pocket and dialed Conner's number, waiting impatiently for him to answer. When he did, she didn't even wait for him to say anything before she gasped out six words breathlessly.

"It's Louis! And he has Jaz!"

seventeen

"Who on earth?" Conner nearly screamed into the phone.

"Jaz! Jasmine!" Violet sounded nerve-wracked.

"*Who* has Jaz?" Conner did scream this time.

"Louis! Louis Staunton!"

"Who the—oh, oh no WHAT!"

It took Conner a few seconds to remember who Louis Staunton was. And with the revelation came decades-old memories of fighting, violence, fear, and pain.

Louis Staunton had been Violet's third bodyguard back when she'd was Violet Arnnu—the leader of the Violet Army.

There had always been some competition between Conner and Louis. They had clashed during the attack on Encephalon, and Louis had been the one to shoot Conner's best friend, Jack Marwick. He'd seemingly melted out of the picture after the Purple Blitzkrieg was over...but here he was again. And targeting the Whyte family—

Conner's blood ran cold. They had to rescue Jasmine!

"Conner, I'm going to hang up, and I'm going to call the police," Violet told him, her voice a bit less frantic now. "I got the license plate number."

"Wait," Conner interrupted. "You're *sure* he has Jaz? How?"

"Are you kidding me!" Violet screamed. "I saw him! And he saw me! And I don't know why he—" Her voice broke off.

"Okay, go ahead," Conner returned hastily. "I'm going to call Moira. Which direction did they go? I'll see if I can follow somewhat."

"East," Violet replied immediately. "And speeding."

"Okay." Conner nodded a couple of times, though she couldn't see him. "Okay."

"See ya," Violet added. "We'll find her, Conner."

"Right. See you."

Conner hung up and stared in shock at the dashboard for a few seconds before calling his twin sister. This had to be some kind of nightmare. Louis—alive, vengeful, and local.

* * *

"You mean to tell me that that Staunton person is around here, kidnapped Jaz, and escaped?" Moira sat down rather suddenly.

"Yes, that's exactly it," Conner shouted, his phone on speaker and on his lap as he drove. "So keep the other three inside this time, please."

"Conner, when will you figure out how to keep you and your kids out of trouble?" Moira had to ask.

"Moira, I don't know—I'm driving right now, okay!" Conner gritted his teeth as he narrowly missed landing himself in a severe car accident. "I'll call you later. Just keep the kids inside. Got to go."

"Drive safely," Moira muttered as he hung up without waiting for an answer. She sighed, and stared at her phone for a moment before dropping it on the table and standing up.

"Ali, Charles, Evolet!" she called. "Come in here!"

"Coming," came Evolet's voice from his bedroom.

Moira's forehead wrinkled in worry as Evolet came running into the room a few seconds later—alone. "Where are Ali and Charles?" she demanded.

Evolet shook his head, taking in his aunt's panicked expression. "I dunno. Why?" he asked, though he could already guess at the answer.

"Are they outside?" Moira's voice rose shrilly.

"Why—yes—I think so—" Evolet stopped as his aunt's eyes fairly flashed fire.

"Why do you kids not ask me before going outside! When did they go out?" Moira interrogated, already running towards the front door.

"Um, just now, I think. What's going on?" Evolet wanted to know.

"Trouble!" Moira called back over her shoulder.

Evolet looked highly interested. "What kind of trouble?" he asked, but Moira was out of earshot.

The teenager glanced at the table, noticing his aunt's phone there for the first time. He felt his own, fifteenth-birthday-present cellphone in his pocket automatically, wondering what might have happened to get Moira so worked up. It wasn't very hard for him to guess, seeing as he already knew about the threats and had some suspicions as to what Conner and Violet had been up to.

He didn't have to wait long before Moira came back, looking extremely flustered.

"I can't see them," she reported breathlessly. "Go catch them for me, will you? And drag them back here. Actually, don't—you're supposed to stay inside. But so are they. Oh, for heaven's sake—"

"What's going on?" Evolet ran his hands through his hair thoughtfully.

"Some Violet Army maniac has kidnapped Jaz, and your parents are off hunting for them, and Ali and Charles have disappeared," Moira summarized briefly.

"Oh." Evolet shrugged and stepped towards the door. "I'll go find Ali and Charles," he volunteered quickly, trying not to look too excited.

"Oh no you don't," Moira stopped him hurriedly, suddenly realizing what she'd done: She had revealed the entire situation to a superhuman fifteen-year-old. "You're staying right here."

Evolet's face fell. "Can't I go help Mom and Dad, then?" he pleaded desperately.

Moira's voice was decisive. "*No*—you have to stay here, Evolet!" Suddenly the wrinkles on her brow cleared. "Joyce is in town. I'll call her."

Evolet watched and listened sulkily as Moira took her phone off the table. A look of boredom and disappointment came over his face.

It was going to be a long night. And what was happening with Jasmine?

* * *

Livia was on her way to ask if she could do homework with her best friend—when she turned a corner and Alison slammed into her suddenly.

Alison stumbled back a foot or so, while Livia tumbled hard onto the pavement. She stared up at the older, stronger girl, noticing Charles standing behind Alison. The two stared back, looking somewhat shocked, but the reaction was only momentary, at least for Alison, who proceeded to glare sharply at her twin's best friend.

"What are you doing running into people!" she exclaimed annoyedly. "Come on, we're in a hurry!"

"I noticed," Livia retorted, picking herself up slowly. "And I wasn't running, either." She brushed her skirt and tights off. "What're you in a hurry for?"

"None of your business," Alison snapped evasively, grabbing her little brother's hand. Charles was still staring wide-eyed at Livia.

"Where's Jaz?" Livia went on immediately, her eyes narrowing.

"Kidnapped!" Charles burst out before Alison could stop him.

"What!" Livia was flabbergasted. "You're kidding, right? This is like when Ali told me she exploded?"

Alison glared daggers at Charles. "No, she's actually kidnapped, and we're going to look for her," the twelve-year-old explained briefly. "So bye."

"Hey, wait a sec, I'm coming," Livia decided suddenly.

It was Alison's turn to stare. "No you aren't, you—"

"Yes, I am, or I'm gonna follow you." Livia crossed her arms defiantly. "Pick one."

"You can't follow us!" Alison tilted her nose derisively.

A half-teasing, half-serious smile came over Livia's face. "Mhmm, I can."

"How?" Alison demanded, chortling.

Livia's smile grew wider. "That's my secret. So—"

"You're too little," Alison told her firmly.

It was a mistake. "I'm the same age as you!" Livia shouted indignantly. "And you've got a nine-year-old right there, if you didn't notice! If you don't just let me come, I'm going to tell your aunt—"

"Okay, okay, fine," Alison interrupted hastily. Somehow she sensed Moira would not be very happy with the would-be rescuers. "You can come," she relented, scowling.

Livia's face was like sunshine. "Yeah!"

eighteen

Hours passed, and night was falling over Annapolis. In a small room, underground somewhere, a young girl was waking up.

The first sensation that broke through her unconsciousness was a dull sting in her wrist. It was quickly going away, but gradually she became more and more aware that she felt distinctly out of place: lying on a cold, hard floor. The draft chilled her, despite her jacket and form-fitting running boots. Her hair was messy, and there was a small cut on her cheek that had bled a bit but was now closing up quickly.

Slowly, she opened her eyes, taking in her surroundings while she mentally reviewed the events leading up to her being there. She'd slammed into that car—there had been a moment of shock—and the driver had shoved her in the back seat, stabbing something into her wrist. She'd blacked out immediately.

And here she was now, in this tiny, concrete-floored room with reinforced wooden walls, all alone.

Jasmine stood up, blinking, and glanced down at her wrist. There was just a tiny scar there now, and she could assume that it had something to do with her sudden unconsciousness.

But where was she?

There was a door, she noticed: a thick, heavy-looking affair. Tiptoeing over to it carefully, in case someone was on the other side, she wrapped her hands around the knob as tightly as she could, and tried to open it. But, as she'd expected, it was locked.

Sighing resignedly, she retreated to the other end of the room, and then charged the door, throwing herself at it recklessly.

"Oww!" she yelped an instant later, having succeeded only in making herself feel somewhat sick, as well as bruised. That wasn't going to work.

So she tried her last resort: screaming at the top of her lungs. "Hey! Let me out of here!"

There wasn't an answer, but Jasmine hadn't really been expecting one. With a small, grim smile, she glanced around herself again, tensing as she thought she heard something.

She held her breath, waiting. There it was. Footsteps, coming from above her.

If only she could climb up to the ceiling and listen somehow! Jasmine frowned, but then she realized the ceiling wasn't that high after all. Maybe—

She ran over to the wall, leaning her ear against it, still holding her breath as she listened as well as she could. Her ears were good at picking up sounds, and with the physical contact for vibration sensing, she could hear a voice. If she strained her ears, she could hear what it was saying.

"I'm giving you half an hour, Trooper. Then it'll be too late."

Silence. Jasmine remembered that "Trooper" had been basically another name for her father at one point, and her forehead furrowed in confusion. But since there wasn't a reply, maybe whoever was talking was speaking with her father on the phone?

Then there was the voice again. "Right—I'll see you soon." The voice—it was a man's—laughed, and Jasmine had a creepy sensation that it was an insane laughter. "Remember, you can't call the cops. Goodbye, A1."

A short pause. Footsteps again. Jasmine froze as the sounds faded away gradually, her mind racing. Who was upstairs?

What did they want with her? And what about her dad?

* * *

"Aunt Moira, please," Evolet begged for the thirtieth time that hour, the two hundredth time that day. "Let me go help!"

"Evolet, I said no." There was a stressed edge to Moira's voice that brooked no further discussion. "Stop. Do your homework."

"I finished it hours ago," the teenager protested quickly. But Evolet knew he wasn't going to win this argument.

"Go read a book or something," Moira insisted. She fixed him with a glare. "If you go outside, Evolet—I will tell your father."

Evolet nodded silently, disappearing from the kitchen doorway.

Moira breathed a small sigh of relief.

It was nine o'clock at night. The two had skipped dinner, with Moira calling Joyce almost constantly to see if she'd found Alison and Charles yet—which she hadn't. Moira didn't dare go out herself because she knew Evolet would follow—and she didn't want Evolet to follow. First of all, Conner had asked her to keep all the kids inside—and second of all, she was afraid she'd lose Evolet. Maybe it wasn't fair, but she knew she loved him and needed him more than any of his siblings. Of course, she loved them too. But if she were to lose Evolet—

Suddenly she became aware of knocking at the door, and Evolet shouted that he'd get it.

"No, you don't—I will," she yelled, standing up quickly without bothering to push her chair back in. As she rushed to the door, she heard Evolet's starting to say something about his being a whole fifteen years old.

Sitting on his bed boredly and conscientiously holding a book, Evolet listened carefully as his aunt opened the door.

"Hello?" she asked. Someone said something; the voice was a new one for Evolet, and he couldn't hear what they said, but obviously

Moira did, for she went on with: "What business is that of yours?"

A new voice answered, and Moira gasped sharply.

Evolet's eyebrows shot up as the door slammed shut a moment later. Less than thirty seconds afterward, he heard a car driving away from the front of the house, and suddenly a suspicion struck him.

"Aunt Moira?" he called. There was no answer.

"Aunt Moira!"

Still nothing.

Evolet threw the neglected book onto his bed, leaping onto the floor. His sneakers and jacket were already on; they'd been on for hours.

It was a matter of seconds for him to tear through the house looking for Moira, though he already knew he wouldn't find her inside.

Breathlessly, he ran out onto the front porch after his search, and looked around. It was extremely dark, and even with his extraordinarily good eyes he couldn't see Moira anywhere near the front of the house.

Evolet hesitated an instant, then pulled his phone out of his pocket and dialed his aunt's number. She was taking forever to answer, and suddenly he realized she might not have her phone with her. He stepped back into the house, and had his suspicions confirmed: her phone was still on the dining room table.

Evolet ran in and picked it up, hanging up on himself. But his aunt's phone started ringing again, and he glanced at it in surprise. "Conner" was calling.

The fifteen-year-old answered the call, bringing the phone up to his ear. "Hey, Dad," he spoke quickly, "this is Evolet. Dad, what's going on? Aunt Moira just disappeared!"

"What do you mean disappeared?" Conner demanded, but he didn't wait for an answer. Evolet noticed he sounded incredibly strained. "Okay, then, Evolet—do you know what's going on?"

"I can guess," Evolet muttered.

"Huh?"

"The kids got kidnapped?" Evolet guessed.

"No—just Jaz, thus far. That means Joyce hasn't found Ali and Charles yet?"

"Didn't know she was looking for them," Evolet admitted.

"Okay. Well, Evolet, I don't know why, but Joyce isn't answering the phone. I'm about to go into a no-service zone and I don't have any more time. You have to give a message to Joyce for me, okay?"

Evolet's eyes flitted around, looking for a scrap piece of paper. He spotted one on the other end of the table, and pounced on it, grabbing a pencil out of his pocket at the same time. "Ready!"

"Louis Staunton is in an abandoned shed just outside the city, near the harbor. It's in its own little area, with no other buildings nearby, and there's a big, wooden 'For Sale' sign out front. That's all Staunton will tell me; he says I can't miss it. Got that?"

Evolet's fingers were moving like lightning. "Got—it," he grunted.

"Okay. I have half an hour to get there and I can't be late. He has Jaz. Tell Joyce to rush there as soon as she can. I don't know what's gonna happen. Ev—I think he's insane," Conner went on, his voice getting slightly quieter.

"Huh?" Evolet perked up. "Who?"

"Louis. Do you know who—"

"Yeah, I think," Evolet interjected, remembering the documentary. "Okay. Okay. What's he gonna do? Why'd he tell you he has Jaz?"

"He wants me to meet him," Conner explained. "I might as well tell you everything, till I lose signal at least. He just says he wants me to come, and if I don't, then he's going to—" A pause. "Hurt Jaz," Conner finished, very quietly this time.

"So we're on the way there," Violet's voice cut in faintly. "And we can't call the police."

Evolet smiled slightly upon hearing his mother's voice, despite the gravity of the situation. "Okay, so... I just tell Aunt Joyce to go to that place you described and help out?"

"Yes," Conner returned.

"Dad, can't *I* help?" Evolet asked eagerly. "I could look for Aunt Moira or something? Or I could come, too?"

"Actually, Evolet, what I really need you to do now is—"

And Conner's phone lost signal.

"Oh, *shoot!*" Evolet nearly screamed. "Dad! Dad, are you still here?" he shouted into the phone, listening to the brief cracking noise before it hung up.

He called back, tapping the table impatiently as the phone rang for half a minute and then gave up.

"Of course!" he sighed, wondering what his father had been about to say.

He stared dismally at his phone for a few seconds before calling Joyce, hoping she'd answer. Which she didn't.

For the next five minutes, he tried again and again, and finally he got through.

"Hey Evolet, what's up?" Joyce asked quickly.

"Aunt Joyce, Dad wanted me to let you know where he's headed to. He found Jaz—sorta." Evolet proceeded to give the description. By the time he was finished, Joyce was gasping.

"So it's Louis! That brute!" she exclaimed. "Well, I'll be on my way. Thanks, Evy. Bye."

"Goodbye," Evolet replied hastily, glad that she hadn't given him any injunctions as to staying inside or anything of the sort. Aunt Joyce wasn't usually the type for that, which was a good thing, because Evolet had other plans right now.

He bent down quickly, checking to make sure that his shoes were still tied tightly. Seeing that they were, he straightened and slipped his phone securely into his pocket, zipping up his coat all the way. The next moment he was tearing out the door like a madman and bolting down the dark and deserted street.

nineteen

"Let go of me, right now!" Moira started yelling as soon as she was capable of doing so, having been abruptly kidnapped, promptly silenced, and hustled into a waiting car by her abductors, two darkly dressed young women who'd asked her quietly if this was the Whytes' home.

Now the car was driving off quickly. Moira was being held in a seat by the door, someone holding her hands tightly behind the seat. Sitting in the seat across from her was one of the women; behind her was the other. A third sat in the front passenger seat. A man was driving, and another sat in the backseat, diagonal from Moira.

She counted them quickly: there were five of them. Definitely too many for her alone.

"Shh," the woman sitting behind her cautioned. Moira couldn't see much of her in the dark, but her voice sounded about twenty years old. "Who are you?"

"What do you mean, who am I?" Moira struggled to keep her voice strong and calm-sounding. "Who are you and what do you want?—I'm going to call the cops!"

"You haven't got your phone with you," the woman sitting across the aisle remarked dryly. She was fishing something out of her pocket, and now she pulled out a flashlight, immediately shining it at an angle to Moira so she could see her face. Moira quickly got a glimpse of her kidnappers as well.

"Oh, you're Moira Whyte," the woman observed, a keen look of disappointment crossing her face. "What a pity. Well, at least it explains how we got you in here."

"What are you talking about?" Moira hissed, angry at having her identity so easily revealed.

The woman—probably over her mid-twenties, with dark hair and skin, and a pair of glasses—smiled wryly, and ignored the question.

"Who is at home with you? Petyr, looks like we'll have to go back."

"Whatever," the driver muttered. He was probably thirty, with light brown hair and green eyes, and was dressed in dark clothes like the others.

"Why do you think someone's at home with me?" Moira demanded heatedly, hoping she could keep these people away from Evolet. "What with my brother and his wife chasing after a kidnapper—and the other kids disappeared—"

The older of the two dark-haired women tensed visibly. "What? Nobody's at home but you?"

"Someone got kidnapped?" the young man in the back seat asked in disbelief. "Huh?"

"Explain," the driver commanded gruffly.

"We can probably help," the woman in the passenger seat added.

Moira allowed herself a tiny, tight smile. "Help how? Who are you?"

The five—well, the four that weren't driving—exchanged glances.

"Depends on who the enemy is," the man in the back seat replied for them all.

"Louis Staunton," Moira revealed, and immediately her hands were released. She put them on her lap, smiling wryly.

"Then we're on your side," Petyr declared. Moira saw the woman closest to her smile in a way that Moira found unsettling.

"So you're Moira?" the girl in the back seat asked. "Can we call you that? Or do you prefer Miss Whyte? I'm Riley."

"Call me Moira," Moira shrugged, feeling relieved that her kidnappers were apparently against Louis as well. She wasn't sure yet if she was going to trust them, but for now she could play along. "Hi Riley."

"Petyr," the driver spoke up.

The woman in the passenger seat interrupted with, "She already knows that... I'm Flynnette, or Flynn."

"Tina," the one closest to Moira introduced herself. "Well, Christina," she added conscientiously, "but Tina for short."

"And I'm Jason," the young man in the back seat finished quickly.

"So where do we start looking for the kidnappers and kidnapped?" Petyr demanded gruffly. "And Staunton, naturally."

Moira relaxed some of her tension. This was looking vaguely like the real thing, even if her companions weren't saying much about how they'd come there or why they'd kidnapped her.

"I guess we can just cruise for now," she decided.

"What are we looking for?" Tina wanted to know.

"Three groups. First one: nine-year-old boy and twelve-year-old girl—" Moira began.

"Charles and... Alison or Jasmine?" Jason broke in.

"Alison." Moira raised her eyebrows at their obvious knowledge of the Whyte family, but otherwise gave no sign of her surprise. "Secondly... Violet and Conner. I expect you know them."

"Who doesn't?" Riley chortled from the backseat. Tina muttered something in reply.

"And third?" Petyr inquired.

"Thirdly, Louis Staunton and Jasmine," Moira finished.

"Okay. Totally can't miss 'em," Flynn grinned from the passenger seat. "So if you do, Petyr—"

Petyr cut her short by turning suddenly to avoid crashing. "I will miss them, but I won't miss a collision if you don't..." His voice trailed off. Clearly, he was paying more attention to the road than anything else.

"Okay, whatever," Flynn muttered.

Moira smiled slightly, getting the impression that the two were siblings.

"How long is this gonna take?" Jason wanted to know.

"Dunno," Petyr returned. "Cruise 'round till we find 'em. That's orders."

"Whose orders?" Moira questioned softly, more to herself than to anyone else.

But Riley heard her. She clenched her fists discreetly.

No one noticed.

twenty

"That's it. That's got to be it."

Violet leaned forward slightly in the passenger seat to point at the shed, a tumble-down affair with a for-sale sign in front and a dusty light on in front of the door.

Conner slammed his foot on the brakes, bringing the car to a sudden yet controlled stop in front of the house.

He stared at the shed for a moment. A look of hard, determined resolve flashed across his face as he grabbed his gun from the glove compartment. "Let's go deal with that—Staunton."

Violet nodded silently, and followed his example. But just before they both hopped out their respective doors, she paused and glanced at her husband. He looked back, waiting for her.

They nodded to each other, smiling slightly.

"Let's go get Jaz," Violet whispered.

Conner saluted. "Spot on. Let's go."

A few seconds later, they marched away from the car and towards the house, keeping an even pace with each other.

Conner's smile turned grim.

They stopped in front of the dilapidated front door, Conner's hand on the knob.

"If only we knew Joyce was on her way," he muttered.

Violet tilted her head, and looked at him. "We can handle this, Conner. Come on, you've still got the old, fearless Trooper in you somewhere, right?" she demanded, smiling playfully.

Conner shrugged. "I guess. But—"

"Just think of Jaz, and let's head in," Violet told him confidently.

That did it, and Conner's chin set solidly. Without answering, he turned the knob, and the door opened.

He and Violet stared inside the single room in surprise. It was empty; but there was another door across the room. They walked inside, and looked around cautiously before approaching the second door.

Conner rested his hand on the doorknob, gesturing to Violet with his other hand. He counted silently.

Three. Two. O—

A sixth sense alerted him, and he glanced up, just in time to see a black shape dropping out of the ceiling onto him. He shouted, and stepped aside, but too late; the next instant he was tangling with a desperate, T4-ified Louis Staunton.

"Die!" the older man yelled, knocking the gun out of Conner's hand and pinning him to the ground. Taken by surprise, Conner stared up into a dark, twisted face filled with hate.

"I will kill you," Louis hissed vengefully, his eyes burning. "You can't get away with what you did, you yellow, upstart traitor—"

Conner twisted suddenly and powerfully, knocking Louis to the hard, concrete floor. "*You* are the traitor," he returned quickly, trying not to let his temper get the better of him as he jumped to his feet, keeping Louis down on the floor with one foot. Conner was younger, and stronger too. "You betrayed America! Vi—go get the cops."

"Don't go anywhere," Louis spat from the floor as Violet turned to go. She paused, and stared at him as he continued: "You shouldn't have joined them, Trin."

"That's not my name," Violet interrupted, her purple eyes flashing, but Louis wasn't done.

"You know you're as guilty as the rest of us were," Louis continued, with a maniacal gleam in his eye. "And worse. Your father—"

"Shut up," Conner broke in sharply, pressing down harder. "Vi, go get the cops," he repeated. Violet nodded, her face turning white as Louis started yelling.

"Yeah, go get the cops! By the time you get back everyone you love will be gone—"

Conner shouted in surprise as Louis moved suddenly, grabbing something from his pocket. He waved it in the air victoriously, his hand on the small red button. Violet gasped, but Louis laughed insanely.

"Get away from me, Trooper! Or I will blow this place sky-high!"

Conner hesitated, but as he looked at Louis he knew the man would actually do it.

He sucked in a breath, doubt written all over his face.

"First, where's Jasmine?" he demanded heatedly.

"Downstairs," Louis replied, laughing wildly. "Ground zero. Let me up, Conner, or we can't talk properly."

"Okay," Conner agreed reluctantly, stepping back. He backed up to the wall, and looked discreetly at the door, realizing it was probably a stairwell.

He started slightly as Violet slid her hand into his, and he looked at her. She seemed determined, though she was still flushed. He squeezed her hand reassuringly.

"You told us to come here," he reminded Louis, who was still brandishing his detonator triumphantly. "Why'd you kidnap Jasmine only to ask us to come here?"

"I wanted you to come," Louis replied, a cunning smile spreading over his face. "You especially. Look, I'll let Trin and your little girl go—if you, Trooper, stick around, and Trin stays out of this mess. I told you I'd get revenge someday."

"You can't do this," Violet began angrily, but Conner held up a hand.

"What if we say no," he suggested.

Louis laughed. "Then I detonate the explosives," he countered triumphantly. "And *nobody* survives."

"Conner—" Violet gasped.

"Let Jasmine go," Conner commanded firmly.

Louis nodded, crossing the room to the second door in a few long steps. He opened it slowly and slid his hand along the inside wall.

They could hear a door opening, and then footsteps. A few seconds later, Jasmine came running out—and Louis grabbed her firmly by the hand. She gasped, and stared at her parents across the room. Violet and Conner looked very much like running over, but Louis was still holding the detonator.

"Now," he began, "I'm going to finally get my revenge."

He let go of Jasmine, and pulled something else out of his pocket: a short, slightly curved purple-tinted crystal knife with a fine, lethal tip.

Violet's eyebrows shot up as she caught Jasmine in her arms, but Conner ignored Louis, smiling at Jasmine and whispering gruffly that everything was going to be alright.

"Dad, Mom, what's going on?" Jasmine demanded.

Conner looked down at her and pushed her hair out of her face fondly. He lost a bit of his smile as he took in the small cut on her cheek.

"Stay with Mom," he told her quietly. "You're gonna be okay."

"Conner," Violet put in softly, "what are you doing? You can't just—"

"Are you kidding me?" Conner whispered back, glancing momentarily at Louis, who was still on the other side of the room. "Of course I'm not just gonna let him do whatever. I'm going to fight. But you have to keep Jaz—and the others—safe. Now that we know what he wants."

Jasmine's ears perked up. "Hey, Dad, I can fight too," she told him rashly. "Can I help?"

Conner's face broke into a grin, and he actually laughed aloud. "No—stay with Mom," he told her again.

"Conner, I can't let you do this alone. He's dangerous." Violet's face was white. Her purple eyes looked strangely tired and pained, and her short dark brown hair was something of a mess.

She held Jasmine tightly, kneeling on the ground so Jasmine was just about as tall as her. The two watched Conner anxiously.

He laughed lightly again, trying to make them feel better. "I'm not alone while you're here, and anyway, I've beaten him before. I'll do it again. Just stay with Jaz."

"Okay," Violet agreed finally. She swallowed hard, and nodded.

Louis walked away from the opposite wall and towards them, also watching

Conner. He'd lost his maniacal grin, and now he just stared out of crazily flashing gray eyes.

Conner stepped away from his wife and daughter and watched Louis intently as he toyed with his knife in one hand and the detonator in the other.

"I have been practicing this for five years," Louis began happily, an odd, creepy smile coming over his face. "And now—finally—"

He held the knife in throwing position, pausing as he realized that Conner wasn't looking quite at him. But that lasted for only a second, and then he met Louis's gaze again. Louis was much gratified to see a look of something like fear in those hated deep blue eyes.

"Finally," he whispered maniacally, and drew his hand back.

But, like twenty years before, he never got a chance to actually throw it.

Someone jumped him suddenly from the doorway, light but fast, and brought him to the ground with a *thud*.

The knife clattered away on the concrete floor, and Louis held desperately onto the detonator as a fourteen-year-old T4-ified boy landed on top of him, kicking away furiously, and shouting: "You stay away from my dad and sister!"

"Evolet!" Jasmine screamed.

twenty-one

Evolet tackled Louis with a strong football move, slamming him into the floor. He managed a short gasp of victorious laughter as he jumped away lightly, having disarmed the older, stronger man.

Louis got to his feet, still holding the detonator, and suddenly Evolet noticed the device for the first time. He dove for it, but Louis caught him and held it aloft, trying to kick Evolet away from him.

Evolet dropped and grabbed hold of the man's lower legs, trying to knock him down again. Louis kept kicking, but Conner was back, shoving Louis against the wall and reaching for the detonator.

Louis fumbled with the detonator, but in his desperate frenzy, some of his fingers weren't quite working, and he panicked, throwing the detonator as hard as he could out the open door in hopes it would smash and set off the explosives.

Conner froze, missing the catch.

Evolet reached up from his sudden seat on the floor, but it went too high for him, out the door, into the blackness—

There was a moment of horrified silence. Evolet found himself staring at Jasmine, both their faces white in mute terror and shock.

Louis actually stopped fighting Conner, and the both of them fell back from each other, holding their breaths and waiting for the explosion that was certain to come.

It seemed an eternity later when they heard a voice from the darkness outside, and someone stepped up the front steps into the light from the house. He looked about twenty, Conner noticed immediately; his longish, slightly messy hair was a curly light brown. He had a sharp chin that reminded Conner of someone as he called out, "Hey, cool thing here. I wonder what happens if I press the—"

He had caught the detonator. They were saved.

"Do it," Louis interrupted him, his face dark with hateful passion.

He and the darkly-dressed newcomer stared at each other for a moment, and then the twenty-year-old young man tilted his head slightly to the side, and shook his head. "On second thought...maybe it's not such a good idea."

"Move," someone cut in from behind him as five more people crowded inside.

Conner stepped away from Louis, whose eyes were staring out of his head as he realized the battle was lost; Conner smiled at Moira as she came in behind the young man. Conner's sister looked somewhat flustered but was otherwise her usual self. She glanced at Evolet, and her eyebrows shot up.

A guilty flush crept into Evolet's cheeks. He got up and went over to his mother and Jasmine. Violet hugged him tightly, and stood up as well; Evolet held out a hand for Jasmine, and she took it, and got to her feet, smiling trustingly at her older brother.

They backed up to the wall together, silently watching Louis as his face contorted in rage. Then Evolet's gaze shifted to the five strangers, and he took them in curiously.

There were three that looked like siblings, the two men and one of the girls. The young woman seemed to be of an age between her brothers. The younger man's eyes were a light, cheerful grayish brown, and so were his sister's. Their older brother's were a dark green hue.

All three of them were dressed similarly, in dark jackets complete with hoods, and black leather form-fitting boots.

Then there were the other two, both of them Asian-looking, with dark hair skin. The older woman was dressed in a smart, business-like way, but the younger one had a longer skirt, and a more casual jacket.

Evolet realized that the first woman, the one with the two brothers, was watching him and Jasmine intently, with a tiny hint of a smile on her face. He looked away with difficulty after a moment. Her stare was making him nervous.

"Moira!" Conner exclaimed. "What are you doing here? Who are these people? Hey, can I have that please—" he broke off, seeing that the twenty-year-old was still holding the detonator as if he were about to set it off.

The younger man handed it over, a sheepish grin coming over his face.

"They're friends—I guess," Moira added, dropping her voice to a whisper that only her brother could hear. His eyebrows shot up.

"Conner Whyte?" the older man asked, stepping over to him. He extended a hand. "I'm Petyr. Nice to meet you."

After a brief moment of hesitation, Conner shook his hand hard, reassuring himself that whoever this man was, he did not have the T4 injection—something the man's strong build had made him suspicious of.

Conner allowed himself a smile. "Yeah, that's me. Looks like you guys stepped in in the nick of time there."

"It's fine, we look out for each other," the younger man told him, smiling openly. He shoved his older brother aside playfully and took his turn shaking hands. "Hey, Mr. Whyte. I'm Jason."

Conner was about to say hello when he heard the whir of sirens outside, and suddenly another head popped through the doorway, a Middle Eastern one, with olive-toned skin, short blackish hair, and lively dark eyes.

"I got the cops," the newcomer announced needlessly, glancing over the room's inhabitants. "Whoa! What a crowd!"

"Hi, Joyce." Moira and Violet grinned at the same time. Violet ran forward the next moment as Alison, Livia, and Charles pressed forward to see the "crowd," revealing their presence. The young mother scooped her children both into a tight hug, lecturing and explaining in the same breath.

Moira contented herself with glaring at her niece and nephew until they felt her eyes on them and looked up to see a very angry and severe-looking aunt glowering at them. Alison shrugged it off, but Charles froze, staring back at Moira with wide eyes.

Evolet repressed a smile. He'd thought Moira was just as scary when he himself was nine. And sometimes she was just that scary.

Meanwhile, Livia watched the proceedings, gaping with her mouth hanging wide open.

Joyce directed the police in, and they took Louis with them, while Evolet realized that the man was staring at him out of flashing gray eyes.

The boy tensed, and his smile disappeared as Louis hissed at him. "I will kill you too."

Evolet jumped when Conner tapped his shoulder, and he breathed a sigh of relief to see it was just him.

"You alright?" Conner asked him simply, but their eyes spoke volumes.

Evolet nodded simply. "Is he—"

"Evy, it'll be fine. They won't let him get away, even if he is insane," Conner assured him. "We're all going to be safe now. Thanks to you," he added, grinning. "That was great timing."

"It may have been great timing, but I think I told him to stay inside," Moira broke in, and Evolet discovered she was standing right next to him.

"I—" and he flushed again. "But you disappeared," the fifteen-year-old added quickly.

Moira coughed. "Well, that was—" she choked, turning around to hide her face.

Evolet grinned helplessly and glanced at Jasmine, who was laughing. Conner watched them, smiling, for a moment, but one of the policemen wanted to talk to him, so he stepped away.

"Evolet, that was really amazing," Jasmine whispered to her older brother, her eyes shining.

Evolet laughed nervously, and made to answer, but then suddenly he and Jasmine became aware of a third presence. Evolet turned to see the woman who had been staring at them. Now she was just behind them—for some reason, she'd stepped around.

Evolet stared back at her, silently. She smiled slightly.

"You're Evolet Whyte?" she asked softly, and Evolet nodded. "I'm Flynn. Nice to meet you."

"Isn't that a..." Jasmine began, her voice dropping and becoming inaudible suddenly.

"Isn't that a boy's name?" Evolet finished for her.

But Flynn ignored the question. Instead she was looking at Jasmine. "Hey, is she alr—" she started.

Evolet felt Jasmine's hand he was holding go limp. Startled, he turned to look at her as well, and held her up as she slipped forward towards the floor without warning.

Evolet's eyes widened in shock as he saw that his sister's face was white and pale.

"Dad!" he shouted.

<h1 style="text-align:center">twenty-two</h1>

"What? Jaz?" Evolet burst out, any hints of a smile vanishing from his face as he held his sister up.

Her face was completely blank. Her eyes closed.

"Jaz!" Evolet shook her. Nothing changed.

"Evolet, what's—" Conner's voice broke off as he saw Jasmine's face and realized what was happening. Quickly he picked her up, lifting her easily into his arms. He studied her face anxiously. "Vi—"

"Oh, heavens, Conner, let's get her to the hospital right away," Violet exclaimed, taking in the scene instantly. "What happened?"

"Evolet?" Conner asked, glancing down at his eldest.

Evolet held his hands out questioningly, his purple eyes frightened. "I dunno, Dad—she just suddenly dropped—"

"Probably something Louis did," Violet interrupted, her own matching eyes flashing fire. "Come on, Conner, let's go. Ali! Charles! Evolet! Get into the car. Moira—"

"There's only one time I've ever seen someone like that," Moira breathed, biting her lip as she looked at Jasmine.

Two minutes later, the Whytes were packed into their car. Conner glanced out the window; Joyce was trying to talk to the mysterious five.

"Door," Conner grunted, and Charles leaned out to slam it shut. But then, just before he was about to start the engine, Conner heard tapping out the passenger window. Glancing over, he noticed that the girl who'd called herself Flynn was trying to get their attention.

Sighing, Conner motioned to Evolet, who rolled down the passenger window. The teenager was sitting in the passenger seat, and now he leaned back somewhat, letting his father get a clear view of the third party.

"Hey, Mr. Whyte," Flynn began, casually, "can I catch a ride to the hospital? I wanna know that she's gonna be okay." She jerked her head in the direction of the middle seat, where Jasmine slumped between her mother and Alison, still unconscious.

Conner's eyebrows shot up, but he wasn't about to refuse, and he wanted to know more about the five. "Sure," he shrugged, and glanced at Evolet. "Can you vacate that seat?"

Evolet gave Flynn another, hard look, wondering again where he'd seen that easy, nonchalant air. He scrambled out of the passenger seat into the back row, where Charles was falling asleep.

"Hey, bro," he greeted him as he buckled himself in.

Charles's eyes flickered open, and he smiled slowly. "Hi Evolet. You know what? That was really cool."

"Huh?" Evolet asked him in surprise.

"You're really cool," Charles mumbled sleepily.

"Oh, okay," Evolet returned, staring in surprise at his younger brother from whom he'd never heard anything but challenges before. "Thanks."

"Yeah, you're amazing," came another voice from the seat in front.

Evolet looked up, only to see Alison's smirk. "But Imma be cooler than you," the twelve-year-old hastened to assure her older brother awkwardly. "Someday."

Evolet's face cracked into a giant grin. He turned to look at Moira, who sat quietly on the other end of the back row. She smiled back, a look of reluctant pride coming over her face.

"Don't get too big for your boots, now," she warned him, her eyes twinkling.

"Like my kids have small boots?" Violet demanded.

"I wasn't aware that Evolet had any boots," Moira responded absentmind-edly.

Violet began muttering something that she kept to herself, but Evolet tried in vain to keep from grinning. It was useless, and he was glad when the car lights turned off and Conner started driving, so no one could see Evolet's face.

He grinned helplessly at the floor.

He was worried about Jasmine, but he was happy, too. It seemed his other siblings had finally accepted him!

* * *

At the hospital, Conner got someone to stay in the car with sleeping Charles, and all the other Whytes escorted Jasmine in—Violet carried her, with Evolet following her anxiously, as if, Violet noted, she couldn't keep a good grip on her own twelve-year-old!

But she smiled as she said it, and smiled even harder when Jasmine almost seemed to wake up for a moment, as they got her into triage. Evolet frowned when he noticed Flynn biting her lip—until Alison, who'd suddenly transformed into a caring, worried twin, exclaimed that she wasn't waking up after all.

Evolet was still watching the young woman when they finally got into the room, though he took up a place by the head of the bed immediately. Everyone crowded around, except Flynn, who stood by the window and did something on her phone. Conner and Violet cast glances at her momentarily, but turned to pay attention as a nurse entered and proceeded to inspect the casualty.

"Oh, she's just asleep," the nurse surmised after a few seconds. "What'd you bring her in for?"

"She passed out suddenly," Conner explained, trying not to sound irritated. "She never does that."

The nurse gave him an odd glance, and suddenly her gaze darted to Flynn, who was still by the window. Evolet turned his head quickly to see what they were looking at each other for, but as far as he could see, Flynn didn't pay any attention to the nurse at all, and when he looked back the nurse was using her stethoscope on the twelve-year-old.

"Yeah, she's fine," the woman repeated, shrugging. "But I can check if you want...?"

Violet glanced at Conner, who nodded. "I guess."

"Okay. I'll do that." The woman put her stethoscope away and went over to the hospital room counter, opening a drawer. She pulled out a small syringe, and broke off the protective tip.

Walking back over to the patient, she pulled out a small alcohol prep pad and opened it, dabbing Jasmine's arm a couple of times and putting a band around it. She paused on seeing a couple of reddish marks on the girl's wrist.

"She's been injected with something," she noted aloud, glancing hard at Conner again.

"We noticed," Evolet muttered dryly, as his father didn't make to answer. He was too busy watching as the nurse stuck the needle in Jasmine's arm and proceeded to draw some blood.

Evolet caught his breath. It looked like normal blood, but so much of it made him feel somewhat sick.

When it was his sister's, anyway.

"What are you doing that for?" Violet wanted to know, her eyes narrowing. In the corner of the room, Flynn looked up, her brows furrowed.

"To run tests," the nurse returned shortly. "I'll get back to you in a few minutes," she added as she wiped off Jasmine's arm, put a huge bandage on it, capped the syringe, and headed for the door.

"It took days for them to get results about you," Moira muttered as the nurse left. She looked around for a seat, and noticed the window seat. Flynn sat down there as well, and Alison.

"Who?" Conner blinked.

"You, obviously! I bet they won't be back for awhile," Moira predicted pessimistically. "Maybe a week? But she'll be awake by then, whenever it is, and we can leave." She sighed, crossing her legs as she sat down.

"So you think she'll be fine?" Flynn spoke up, rising suddenly.

"Hopefully," Violet replied, glancing at the younger girl in surprise.

"That's good," Flynn commented, smiling slightly. "But I just checked the time and it's almost eleven. So... I should probably say goodbye."

"Do you have a ride to where you need to go?" Violet wondered aloud. "We can give you a ride when we leave if you like."

"In a week," Moira muttered, but nobody noticed.

"Oh, I'll be fine." Flynn smiled. "I'll see you 'round. Oh, do you want my phone number? I'd like to know if—er—Jasmine, I think?—is alright."

"Sure," Violet shrugged, searching in her purse for a piece of paper.

Two minutes later, Flynn walked out, waving. Violet stored her phone number in her pocket, and looked up abstractly. "This is taking forever."

"Like I said..." Moira was anxious to make her point, but she never finished it.

"So, Aunt Moira, where have you seen someone look like that before?" Evolet asked curiously, staring hard at his younger sister. She still looked completely out.

"Your mother," Moira returned shortly, glancing sideways at Violet.

"What?" Violet asked sharply.

"Remember Joyce?" Moira sighed. "We had to knock you out to save her, and we used that thing they were gonna use on Conner—"

"Oh, the LVK?" Violet remembered. She glanced at Jasmine. "In that case, Jaz is fine. But...LVK is impossible! Doesn't the government have it locked up somewhere?"

"Supposedly," Conner muttered, knitting his brows.

"And how could Louis have given it to Jasmine?" Moira went on. "He was all the way across the room. And if he hates you so much, Conner, why Jasmine and not you?"

"I don't know," Conner admitted. He frowned. "It doesn't really take that long to act. You're right, it couldn't have been Louis. At least, not the second time."

"So—" Moira broke off.

"Who could have done it?" Alison spoke up for the first time. She looked like she was falling asleep.

"The only other person around us was Mom—oh, and that Flynn person," Evolet remembered.

"Flynn?" Violet asked sharply.

Conner frowned harder. "We don't know anything about them," he admitted a few seconds later.

He, Moira, and Violet exchanged glances, Evolet watching them curiously.

"I'll call her tomorrow," Conner decided. "But it's probably nothing. Do the effects recur, Vi?"

"I dunno." Violet shrugged. "I did feel sleepy for awhile afterwards. Maybe my brain wasn't working right, and that's why I joined you guys." She tilted her head to the side thoughtfully.

"You mean it was working right for the first time in your life," Moira corrected dryly.

Violet laughed. "Maybe."

And there was silence as the Whytes watched and waited impatiently for their beloved, sweet-to-the-point-of-fragility Jasmine to wake up.

twenty-three

Evolet thought he would fall asleep himself at this rate, but finally Jasmine stirred on the clean white bed, just as they heard a knock on the door before the nurse marched in.

Evolet had been leaning on the wall, but he bounced back to the side of the bed, watching Jasmine anxiously. Conner, Violet, and Moira did the same, but they looked up as the nurse walked over to them.

"She'll be fine—oh." The nurse looked at Jasmine in surprise as the twelve-year-old opened her eyes sleepily. "She's awake. Well, good. There you go."

"What was it?" Conner wanted to know.

"We found traces of some harmless knockout drug," the nurse answered. "Anyway, I think you can be discharged."

Violet smirked triumphantly at Moira, who frowned. "Back in the day, it would've taken hours, maybe even days, to figure that out," she insisted.

Violet made a gracious gesture. "Welcome to 2041, my dear," she smiled. Moira's eyebrows shot up as she struggled to hide a grin.

Conner gestured to them impatiently, and they fell silent. "So we can leave now?" he asked the nurse, who nodded simply.

"Well, she can wake up a bit more first, of course, but we'll need the room for someone else eventually," the woman told them, thereby implying that they couldn't camp out for more than a few minutes longer.

Alison sighed, and sat up straighter, rubbing her eyes tiredly.

"Okay, thanks," Conner nodded. The nurse ignored him, walking swiftly back out the door.

"What about the bill?" Violet whispered to Conner.

"I'll figure that out," he breezed, stepping over to the bed. "Hey, Jaz. Feeling better?"

"Hi Dad," she murmured. "I guess. What happened?"

"That's what I'm wondering." Conner smiled. He pushed a wisp of light brown hair out of her face gently.

She shook her head. "I don't know."

"It's okay, don't worry about it," Violet broke in. "As long as you're feeling better now."

"I am," acquiesced the girl, sitting up.

Violet laughed, bent down quickly, and kissed her forehead. "That's good. That's great."

"Are we going home now?" Alison demanded from the window seat, not bothering to stifle the yawn that overwhelmed her face.

"I guess," Conner shrugged. He looked back at Jasmine. "If you're sure you're alright."

"Yup," Jasmine assured him. She grabbed Evolet's hand and slid off the bed onto the floor. Bending down, she touched the toes of her boots, then straightened and stretched. "I feel great," she grinned.

"Good." Conner paused and looked around. "Everyone got everything?"

"We didn't bring anything," Evolet noted slowly.

"Then let's go." Conner smiled.

* * *

Evolet nearly fell asleep on the way back home. Maybe he did. It was a long drive. But all he knew was that he suddenly sat up straighter, having heard his name mentioned in the adult conversation. All the other kids were asleep.

"...And Evolet," Conner was saying. "I just hope superkids aren't easily traumatized. But they're still kids. And I remember—"

"I think Evolet will be fine," Moira broke in quietly. "I don't know about Jasmine. But Evolet has never had nightmares or anything before, and I think Jasmine will be the same."

"It's not nightmares I'm worried about," Conner returned. "I mean, Louis literally told Evolet he was going to kill him. That's—"

"They're going to keep Louis contained," Violet broke in. "And here's one thing I know about Evolet: Even if he is the quiet type, he's not going to be afraid of someone like that. He's very confident. He can take care of himself—and he knows it."

Evolet smiled slightly, wondering faintly if he should let them know he was awake.

"Well, then." Conner paused. "But that doesn't solve the problem about who injected Jasmine. Unless the effects recur—but she seemed pretty 'out' to me."

"They might, in a twelve-year-old," Moira suggested cautiously. "The nurse said she found only traces. So maybe it wasn't that recent."

"I don't trust that nurse," Conner muttered. "She should've mentioned that the patient had T4."

"How would she know that?" Violet raised her eyebrows.

"Joyce told me it's on every nationwide test," Conner explained. "The nurse should have known."

"Maybe she recognized us?" Moira wondered. "I mean, maybe she recognized Vi and knew who we were. She would've assumed that we already knew about the T4. Which would be correct."

"Yes, but she still should've brought it up," Conner insisted.

"It's probably fine," Violet decided. "But I want to know more about those five. Why did they kidnap you, Moira? Who are they? Most importantly, *who's giving them orders?*"

Conner nodded. "I'll call them tomorrow. You still have Flynn's number, right, Violet?"

"Yes," Violet returned, not bothering to check her purse. She knew the paper was still there.

"Good." Conner shifted gears and parked the car in Moira's driveway. "Everything will work out fine. We're staying here for the night, right, Moira? It's almost one in the morning."

"Sounds good to me," his twin sister replied, stifling a yawn. "Everything's ready."

Evolet closed his eyes, listening, as Conner put the car into park mode and turned off the engine.

"Okay." Conner nodded to himself. "Let's wake up the kids, shall we?"

twenty-four

"I saw Mom and Dad in the car across the street," Jasmine was telling Evolet the next morning, a Saturday. They were sitting on a high rooftop some distance away from Moira's house.

"That's why I went outside," she continued. "'Cuz I wanted to know if they were watching us. And I guess they were, because I saw Mom come running, just a bit too late," she explained.

"Didn't running into the car hurt?" Evolet asked incredulously. "I mean, I know someone who did that once and they cracked a few ribs."

Jasmine shrugged, and laughed. "Oh, we're hard to kill," she replied pointedly. "And that's the first time I've been to the hospital. Anyway. Mom and Dad seem to think the trouble is over now, don't they?"

Evolet nodded seriously, not in the frame of mind to relate what he'd heard the night before. "They do," he agreed, remembering how earlier that morning he'd heard his parents and Moira talking.

It hadn't quite been on purpose, but he'd overheard them discussing Flynn, Petyr, Jason, Tina, and Riley. Conner had said that he'd tried the number Flynn had given Violet, but that he didn't get an answer.

Then Moira had gotten somewhat worried, but Conner had reassured her that none of the five had T4 and that likely they were just secret government agents looking to deal with Louis, and that that would explain why they had disappeared so promptly after making sure Jasmine would be alright. Joyce had volunteered to make a background check. And Jasmine was 100% better now, so everything was fine. Which Evolet emphatically wanted to believe.

"That's good." Jasmine's voice brought him back to reality as she dangled her legs cheerfully. "That means they'll stop looking so worried, now, right? And Mom will stop talking about moving back to Iceland?"

Evolet had to laugh. "I dunno," he admitted. "But I hope so."

"Perfect," Jasmine beamed. "Just perfect." She leaned back on her elbows, eyeing the gray clouds that threatened snow.

"Think it'll snow before my birthday?" she asked Evolet, with the trusting air of a twelve-year-old girl consulting her older brother.

He smiled. "I bet it will. It always snows in Annapolis in January. As long as I can remember, at least," he corrected hastily.

She giggled. "So January 23? It always snows then?"

Pulling a face, Evolet opened his hands palm upwards in a gesture of utter ignorance. "My memory isn't that accurate," he muttered, arching his eyebrows.

Jasmine smirked. "If you say so," she shrugged. "But I hope it snows. I like snow. You know what? We should have a snow fight. Boys against girls."

He glanced her way, his eyes open wide. "You're volunteering to be on the same team as Ali?" he demanded teasingly.

Her jaw dropped as she realized the implication of what she'd said. "N—o—o!"

Laughter followed as the two continued bantering and then made plans for the twins' birthday party in January.

Jasmine boldly declared that she was going to invite her entire class of thirty-four, most especially Livia—Alison could say what she wanted. Evolet pointed out wryly that they wouldn't have room anywhere at either house for thirty-four kids, whereupon Jasmine suddenly decided the party would be at the city park—hadn't she told Evolet that already? Was he paying attention or not?

And so they talked, ignored and unnoticed by all that passed by—it was just them, the birds, the frigid air, the cloudy, stormy sky: the perfect picture of ideal sibling friendship.

* * *

That picture would have been somewhat marred had its components not been blissfully oblivious of events playing out in the nearby state of Delaware. It was a low, long building out in the country somewhere, a dairy farm on the outside, a network of secret laboratories and offices on the inside. Cows grazed in the fields around it, while inside it that morning a conference was taking place that would greatly affect the Whytes and everyone else involved with the Purple Blitzkrieg twenty years before.

The speaker was a tall man, muscular and well-built, with sparse black hair and bushy dark eyebrows. Across his right eye was a black eyepatch, the same color as his gloves, pants, and boots. There was a scar on his left cheek. Over his gray shirt he wore a dark leather overcoat. His eyes were dark, but they glittered strangely as he looked around him with the wary caution of a veteran fighter.

Though his was the main presence in the room, there were others, about ten of them. Which number included the five who had made contact with the Whytes: Petyr, Flynn, Jason, Tina, and Riley. Four of the other five were simply strong, imposing-looking men; the last was a scientist, it seemed.

They were all seated around a table that was much longer than it was wide, and at one end a small lab kit was set up. Petyr was standing at it, with the other scientist, both of them dressed for work. The dark leader sat at the other end of the table, his eyes shifting around but coming to focus on the two scientists as Petyr began to speak.

"Thanks to Flynn, we got a perfect sample," he began, glancing at the leader. "As you already know, Zaire."

"Right." The man, whose name was apparently Zaire, nodded. "And so? What have we found from it? Go on."

"Nothing yet," Petyr admitted. "But, according to Flynn, it's from one of the superhuman kids. And so it should have T4. Which is what we were looking for."

"It does," Flynn insisted.

"Well, let's see," Petyr shrugged, with a bit of a smile.

He proceeded to uncap a small vial of blood—the sample the nurse had taken from Jasmine the night before. His companion scientist pushed a small slip of tinted paper in front of him and quickly sprinkled a tiny amount of some white powder on it.

Working quickly and carefully, Petyr dabbed a few drops of the blood onto the paper, where it coagulated with the white powder. After a few seconds, the paper's yellowish hue changed to purple.

"Positive for T4," Petyr declared.

"Are there any other tests?" Zaire demanded once the cheering died down. "I want to be sure."

"Well, there is, but..." Petyr hesitated, glancing at his fellow scientist. The man nodded.

"But what?" Zaire persisted.

"Oh, never mind," Petyr sighed. "Flynn? Your finger, please?"

"You used mine last week," Flynn retorted, shaking her head as she crossed her arms stiffly.

"Jason, then." Petyr looked decisively at his younger brother.

"Aww, man," the twenty-year-old protested slowly, "why me? Why must you pick on your siblings, of all people—"

"Just do it," Petyr interrupted impatiently.

Sighing, Jason stood up. "I hate needl—"

He broke off as he realized Zaire was giving him a hard stare. The older man was extremely intimidating, and fear showed in Jason's face.

He pushed his chair in, and walked over to the experiment end of the table resignedly. "Fine."

In the next few minutes, Petyr jabbed his younger brother's finger with a small needle, and Jason held his finger obligingly over the test strip. A small drop of dark blood formed on the tip of his finger, and then it dropped down onto the purple paper.

Jason jumped back with an exclamation of surprise as the T4 suddenly merged with his blood and there was a chemical reaction. The white powder fizzed, and suddenly a light indigo liquid started seeping onto the plastic-covered table.

Petyr stepped back as well, staring first at the experiment and then at his brother. But the next instant the shock disappeared from his face, and he helped his fellow scientist to contain the mess.

"And so," he began waveringly, "obviously something very strong is reacting with Jason's blood."

Jason was staring at the remains of the experiment. "That stuff is not going into me," he muttered, backing away uneasily.

"Oh, of course it isn't going in like that," his brother laughed shakily, though it was obvious he was trying to regain his confidence. "We're going to separate it first. And add our own special touch. And then—"

"And then there will be a victor and there will be a loser," Zaire interrupted, smiling slightly as his dark eyes glittered.

"Be the Victor," Flynn whispered to herself automatically, though she was still watching her brothers. Somehow she sensed Petyr hadn't been expecting that kind of reaction.

Zaire glanced around the table expectantly. Obviously he was waiting for more. An expectation that was met the next moment when every one of the other ten saluted in his direction and roared their slogan.

"We will be the Victors!"

twenty-five

"You guys should know," Petyr was whispering later, in a room alone with his two younger siblings. "That reaction was not expected."

Flynn glanced up at him in surprise from where she was sketching boredly on a piece of paper. "Huh?"

"It shouldn't have reacted like that," Petyr went on, gaining momentum. He looked hard at Jason, who stared back innocently. "I did some more tests. And we're related to that kid you got it from, Flynn."

"What the—?" Jason demanded, jumping up. "We can't be related. We're the only three left in our family—"

"Yeah, but we never found out exactly what happened to the eldest. Remember?" Petyr asked softly, and Flynn's mouth dropped open.

"Grace?" Jason whispered, dropping his happy-go-lucky expression.

Petyr nodded somberly. "Yes. Grace Foley."

The name cut the air like a knife. Petyr bit his lip.

"I never knew her," Jason whispered to himself, but nobody paid any attention to him.

"If Grace is still alive, then she must be—" Flynn cut herself short. She started to say something else, but stopped that as well, and contented herself with staring down at the floor.

"Then she is Violet Arnnu, or Trinity Ryder," Petyr finished for her. "Guys, those kids...have to be our nieces and nephews. What I want to know is: Does this change anything?"

"Change anything?" Flynn echoed. "Why would it change anything?"

"Well, think," Petyr shrugged uncomfortably. "We know Zaire's plan. Or at least part of it."

"Get T4, process T5, discreetly eliminate all those with T4, and then we're free to become the world ruling power," Jason enumerated quietly. "Why does that change anything?"

"Those kids have T4," Flynn told him dryly. "So that means—"

"Can we just tell Zaire to leave them out of it?" Jason suggested after a moment's thought. "They don't have to know anything about us."

"Except they will," Petyr broke in. "Zaire wants a weapon that will wipe out everyone with the T4 strain, instantly. So we could leave the kids and their parents alone, but they'd die anyway." He scratched his chin.

Flynn frowned. "We could give them T5."

"Yeah, but Zaire wouldn't like that, and besides we can't just give them T5, because that'd make them doubly superstrong as well. The premise of Zaire getting rid of all T4s is so that we have no formidable opposition," Petyr pointed out. "I suppose we could put them on our own version of LVED or something like that, but after what happened in the Purple Blitzkrieg I don't think Zaire is going for anything like that."

"But we can't just let the kids die," Jason shook his head. "It's not their fault they have T4. And they're some really good kids,"he added pensively, perhaps thinking of Evolet and Jasmine.

"I think we have no choice," Petyr admitted slowly. "Unless we go to Zaire and tell him the whole thing is off."

"He'd kill us," Flynn spoke up suddenly. "We know too much. And we can't give up now. We're so close."

"But what we *can* do is look for chances to protect the kids," Jason argued. "And maybe Grace, too. Blood is thicker than water, after all."

"Yes," Petyr nodded. "Are we all agreed on that, then? Because we Foleys work together in everything, don't we?"

"Right, we do," Flynn agreed emphatically. "Agreed. We keep working for the Victors, but we also keep an eye out for Grace and the kids."

"Exactly," Jason emphasized.

Petyr managed a smile, and stood up. "Meeting over, then. Gotta get to work on the weapon," he added, somewhat sheepishly. "I shouldn't be here at all."

Flynn laughed. "Okay." She stood up as well, glancing momentarily at the picture she'd drawn. Crumpling it, she tossed it towards a trash can, sighing when it fell short of the mark.

"What are you working on today, Jason?"

* * *

At that same moment, Tina Fletcher was talking to her younger sister, Riley Fletcher. They were the other two of the five that had "helped" the Whytes the night before in order to get their hands on the T4 injection. And now, like Petyr, they had a new assignment. Or Tina did.

She'd gone to look for Riley after she got her assignment, and had finally found her out walking in the cow fields, gathering a small bunch of flowers. Riley heard her sister approach, and she stood up straighter, while Tina marched over to her, a tiny smile on her face.

Riley was only nineteen, and sometimes she shocked her much older sister by acting overly young and feminine as she was doing now. But Riley was just the type for that, Tina reflected to herself. She'd been with the Victors for a few months—only because her older sister was. She'd harden up quickly once things really got started.

"'Sup, Tina?" Riley asked quickly, glancing at her older sister warily.

"I'm going flying, want to come?" Tina's smile brightened. "You've still got some hours yet to earn your PPL."

"Oh, sure," Riley nodded, dropping the field flowers heedlessly and starting to follow her sister back to the main building. "I didn't know we were still working on the PPL," she admitted.

"Well, Zaire says it'll probably take awhile to get things going. And what's wrong with a PPL, anyway?" Tina raised her eyebrows.

Riley shrugged. "Nothing. I don't even know what's going on anymore," she confessed, coming up even with her sister.

"That's fine; I can brief you in the plane, if you like," Tina offered generously, secretly wishing Riley wouldn't seem so confused and out-of-it all the time.

Her sister looked relieved. "I'd love that, thanks."

They fell into step with each other, each young woman lost in her own thoughts. The two reached the building, but Tina only popped inside for a moment to grab a small bag.

"Lunch," she explained, upon Riley's questioning glance. "And dinner. We'll be flying for awhile."

"Oh, fun," Riley grinned. "Anyone else coming?"

"Nope, it'll just be us two, so don't get too excited," Tina warned jokingly. "The destination is Peru—we have to pick up some supplies."

"Cool!" Riley rubbed her hands together in anticipation.

Ten minutes later, they were aboard the small private plane. Riley buckled herself into the copilot's seat, while Tina took the pilot's as a matter of course. It was about fifteen more minutes before they were off the ground, using a conveniently long field as a highway from a "cow-shed" hangar. Riley let the first few minutes pass in silence, watching out the window, before she brought up the subject of the conversation again.

"So. What's going on, exactly?" She frowned. "Nobody ever tells me anything."

Tina didn't mention that *no* newcomers ever got told anything until they passed the initial tests, which Riley had done in Annapolis the night before. And now Tina had permission from Zaire to explain the whole situation to her sister for the first time.

Normally candidates would have a year or so more of probation before being allowed to know the intricate intentions of the Victors, but Riley was Tina's sister, and Tina had been with the Victors for eight years—since she'd been Riley's age, nineteen. So Riley had the green light. And so did Jason Foley, for that matter.

"That blood we got from the Whyte girl?" she began. "It has T4 in it."

"Yeah, I know that," Riley broke in irritatedly. "What of it? Are we getting injected with it or something?"

"Yes, but our scientists have to fix it up first," Tina went on patiently, only half paying attention to her piloting. She was a very good flier, and besides there was no real traffic in the skies anyway. "So they're going to do that, and then we—the Victors—will all get injected. We're going to be superhuman. Not quite as strong as the original T4, but—"

"Why not?" Riley demanded. "Why are we changing it?"

"Stop interrupting," Tina warned her, arching her eyebrows up somewhat. "What happens next is that we release a toxin into the atmosphere that will wipe out everyone with the original T4 and amplify T5. So then we'll be doubly as strong as everyone with T4 is right now."

"Wait, wipe out everyone with the original T4?" Riley blinked. "You mean that entire Whyte family? Why on earth would we do that?"

"It's not just them, it's Joyce Liszt as well, and all the former Violet Army members who are now in prison," Tina enumerated. "But we *have* to do that, so that no one can stop us. Nobody will be *capable* of stopping us. It's that simple," she grinned.

Riley struggled not to clench her fists. She'd suspected something like this.

"But *why* would we do that?" she went on—stupidly, Tina thought. "They haven't done anything to us. And they're a real sweet family."

"Because it's the only way we Victors can get anywhere!" Tina yelled exasperatedly. "Look, Riley, you're—I'm—we're in this to stay. There's going to be a victor when this is all over, and there's going to be a loser." She looked at her sister seriously. "We have to be the Victors."

"But..." Riley's voice faltered.

Tina took one hand off the controls to grip her sister's arm. "We *have* to be the Victors, Riley!"

Riley nodded mechanically. "Fine."

"Say it," her sister insisted.

Riley looked straight ahead as she gritted out the words, now suddenly hateful to her.

"We will be the Victors."

twenty-six

"Have we even got room for seven cups of hot chocolate on us?" Jasmine asked anxiously. "I mean, seriously?"

"Oh, sure," Evolet grinned, fishing some change out of his pocket. "You get three and I'll get four. We can do that."

They were at a popular amusement park in Annapolis. It was the twins' birthday—a Saturday—and the two had finally come to the decision of amusement park, after hours of heated argument, until Conner had threatened they'd spend the entire day at home. So here they were now, two months after the incident, and Jasmine was as well as ever. She and Evolet had decided to get hot chocolates for the family, who were some distance away, at a petting zoo for Charles's sake.

"Here's three-fifty," Evolet told the woman behind the counter, presenting the money with a flourish. "Seven hot chocolates please!"

"Haha, okay," she laughed affably. "Seven hot chocolates coming right up. Give me a couple of minutes."

And with that she grabbed a small stack of cups out from under the counter and began to fill her order.

Evolet and Jasmine grinned at each other, rubbing their hands together to produce warmth. It was snowing, just as Jasmine had hoped, though only lightly, or the park would've been closed. The perfect birthday, Jasmine called it.

"Isn't it so lovely," she chattered, shivering more from excitement than the cold. "I wish it snowed every day."

"We can move to Antarctica when we're grown up, and then there'll be snow everywhere all the time, I think," Evolet suggested cheerfully. "How's that sound?"

"...Cold!" Jasmine giggled, smirking.

Evolet pulled a face.

"Yeah, it'd be extremely cold," Jasmine went on, still smirking. "We'd have to live in an igloo and—"

She paused, realizing that his face was frozen into a perplexed expression as he stared beyond her, at someone or something she couldn't see.

"Evy?"

He didn't answer. She spun around to see what he was looking at.

Someone was pushing their way through the crowd towards the two, someone tall and strong-looking. Her shoulder-length hair—it was light blond at the roots, but apparently dyed black lower down—swung about her darkly tanned face as she elbowed her way past the people around her, her gaze fixed on the two teenagers ahead of her.

Jasmine felt the intensity of the stare, and she, too, froze momentarily.

"Who is that?" she breathed.

"I dunno," Evolet returned, "but let's run." He gripped his younger sister's hand tightly, and they turned together.

"Be right back," he assured the stand manager, who was watching in confusion.

Hot chocolates potentially taken care of, Evolet and Jasmine dashed away together, taking advantage of their youthful size and agility to easily weave their way through the crowd. A hundred feet or so away, they stopped, and Evolet looked around. The woman was still following them, and faster now. She was catching up.

"Wait—" she began to shout above the ordinary amusement park sounds, but Evolet and his sister weren't planning on waiting for an anonymous, seeming superhuman to catch up with them, especially after being cautioned by their parents not to talk to strangers.

"Where are we going?" Jasmine gasped out, being pushed to her utmost speed by her brother's faster limits.

He shook his head. "Mom and Dad?"

"What if—" Jasmine began, then stopped, quite understandably, as her boots caught on some wire on the ground and gravity slammed her down on the pavement. Inertia on the other hand carried Evolet on and beyond before he realized what had happened and managed to stop himself by gripping a pole and swinging around it a couple of times.

"Ow," Jasmine muttered, her face on the ground.

"You okay?" Evolet asked, hopping away from the pole to help his sister up. "Come on, she's coming—"

"Y—e—a—h, I'm fine," Jasmine assured him, grabbing her brother's hand and using it to pull herself up slowly. "I mean I scraped my face and hands and I think my nose is broken—"

"Jaz, just come on," Evolet broke in impatiently. "Are you okay or n—"

"You two," interrupted a voice, and Evolet and Jasmine suddenly realized that the stranger had caught up with them. She was standing a few feet away from the two now, panting hard. "Evolet, and—twin. I need to talk to your parents. Where's your mom?"

Evolet and Jasmine glanced at each other, then back at the stranger, wondering. Should they answer or should they start running again?

The stranger shook her head. There was already a desperate look on her face.

"Look, I need to talk to your parents now. Where are th—"

That was as far as she got. Her question ended abruptly, and she stood rigid for a moment, her hands flying up to her face almost defensively. And then suddenly she dropped to her knees, her hands still partly covering her face. Startled, Jasmine leapt away, while Evolet instinctively stepped forward to support the stranger.

He touched her arm as she knelt, and she jerked it away spasmodically, looking straight at the teenager as she did so. Evolet noticed that her pupils were dilated. A white, pale hue was coming over her face; he guessed she was about twenty.

She stared at him, a burning look in her unnaturally coral-colored eyes.

"Trooper A2," she whispered, and now she fell farther, as if her strength was draining. She held herself up with her hands and managed to lift her head for a last few seconds, to look at Evolet again. "They... They will kill you too."

"Wh—what?" Evolet gasped out, staring back in horror. What was going on?

The stranger couldn't hold herself up anymore. She crumpled to the ground, her face contorting. Her skin was turning a bluish color, but her lips moved to form two last words.

"Zaire. Victors."

"Who?" Evolet asked again, but she seemed frozen there, on the ground.

People were crowding around them, pressing, trying to see what was going on, but Evolet ignored them, though he faintly heard someone calling the police. Kneeling, he leaned forward and suddenly saw a dart in the back of the stranger's neck.

His heart skipped a beat.

She was dead.

Panicking, the teenager backed away slowly, a look of sheer horror on his face.

"Somebody help!" His voice was strangely high-pitched. "Help!"

twenty-seven

It was hours before the Whytes got to their respective homes that evening. First it was at least an hour and a half before they could leave the park, and then they had to go to the police station to testify to what Evolet and Jasmine had seen. The family tagged along, but that didn't help much.

Jasmine and Evolet were a frightened quiet the entire ride home to Moira's house, where Evolet and Moira got out of the car and said goodbye. Evolet was thinking about how the police had dealt with the situation. They'd had a paramedic check the stranger and confirm that she was dead before taking some samples of her blood, her clothing, and the dart. They would try to find out who she had been and who had killed her.

Evolet was also wondering about what the stranger had told him.

Trooper A2. They will kill you too. Zaire. Victors.

It sounded like some kind of warning, he reflected. Why had she called him Trooper A2? Or had she thought she was talking to someone else? Who was "Zaire"? What did "Victors" mean?

There were too many questions, and he was still in a state of shock from having someone die right in front of him. This was nothing like the Louis affair. This was...something different entirely.

One thing he knew was that he was scared. Yes—he, Evolet. He was never scared. But whatever was going on was scaring him. He, and his entire family, had thought everything had changed for the better. But now it seemed it hadn't.

"They will kill you too."

Who? Why?

Completely distracted, Evolet didn't notice his aunt signaling him to follow her into the living room, but instead he started heading into his own room as a matter of course, lost in his own thoughts. Moira turned around and grabbed her nephew's arm, and he looked up, blinking.

"We need to talk," she told him. "Living room?"

"Okay." Evolet nodded mechanically.

Two minutes later found him and Moira settling down in the living room, Moira with a rather serious expression on her face, and Evolet still in a sort of daze.

Moira patted the sofa next to her, and he sat down automatically, still staring straight ahead of him. She snapped him out of that by tapping his shoulder somewhat energetically, and he jumped, and glanced at her questioningly.

"You okay?" Moira demanded, her eyes narrowing as she took in the gray look on his face.

"Y—yeah, I think so," he decided, sitting up straighter and looking her in the eye. "Why?"

"Because when Evolet acts like a ghost—well, he never does," Moira admitted. "You're probably exhausted, though. But it's not quite bedtime yet."

"It's dinner time," he realized. "But I'm not hungry," he added quickly.

His aunt smiled understandingly. "Fed up of interrogation?"

"Ha," he laughed shortly, remembering all the questions the police had asked him and Jasmine. He'd had to answer most of them, because Jasmine had been in a sort of state of traumatic shock.

"Not real interrogation. They knew I didn't do anything—"

"Interrogation all the same," Moira insisted gravely. "Anyway." She paused and licked her lips thoughtfully. "Thoughts?"

"Huh?" Evolet returned, blinking.

"What are your thoughts on the situation?" Moira asked him patiently, sitting back with a light sigh.

"Oh," Evolet breathed, and he ran his hand through his hair. "I... I dunno.

I'm just confused, I guess."

"So am I," Moira had to admit. "So what are you going to do about it?"

Evolet stared frankly. "I *can* do anything about it?"

"Well, I mean: Have you drawn any conclusions?" Moira rephrased slowly.

Her nephew shook his head. "I'm just lost. Aunt Moira, what are Mom and Dad going to do? The woman…she said Zaire would kill us too. Or was it just me? Or…"

Moira shook her head this time, more vehemently than him. "No, there's going to be no more killing. The police are going to find out who was behind this murder, and they're going to take care of it. Got that?" She took a deep breath.

"But they couldn't take care of Louis—Mom and Dad had to do that," Evolet argued. "And even then they almost didn't win."

"Louis was different. Louis had T4 and was insane," Moira reminded him gently. "What, are you scared?"

Her customary smile dropped somewhat as he looked down. "Yeah. Kinda," he confessed. "But… I'm worried about Jasmine too. What if she gets hurt again?"

"I'm glad you're worried about your sister," Moira told him seriously, "but you have got to realize she's super strong, too. You aren't the only one. She can look out for herself."

"Yeah, but…" Evolet's voice trailed off into silence. Moira waited patiently.

And suddenly the fifteen-year-old looked up, straight at her. "Aunt Moira, you knew Mom during the Purple Blitzkrieg, right?"

"Well, yeah," Moira returned, looking somewhat surprised. She tactfully refrained from mentioning that she and Evolet's mother had been enemies— but Evolet probably already knew that. "Why?"

There was an almost desperate look in his purple eyes, eyes Moira had been doubtful of at first but that she had now grown to know and love. "Aunt Moira. Was she a bad guy? I mean a real bad guy? From start to end?" But seeing that his aunt hesitated, Evolet went on: "I mean, did she really turn good in the end? Is she good now?"

"Why are you asking?" Moira asked him frankly.

He frowned slightly. "The documentary we watched at school. It... It said she only turned good because she thought she was gonna lose. But it made Mom look really bad, Aunt Moira," he went on quickly, gaining speed in his anxiety. "Like she is *still* a bad guy. I know that's what my class thinks, at least."

Slowly, Moira shook her head. She'd never thought she'd be the one to have to defend Violet, but she knew there was no way she was going to hold back anything now.

"Your mother was a murderer. You know that, right?" she asked carefully. Her nephew nodded mutely.

"And yes, she was pretty bad. But you know what? She changed. She really did," Moira repeated herself emphatically. "You can believe that."

"A—are you sure?" he breathed.

"Evolet, she could've killed your dad," Moira told him gently. She took his larger hands, and held them tightly as she looked into his purple eyes. "She could've killed him and ended it right then and there. But she didn't."

"The documentary said she was going to lose," Evolet returned confusedly. "She said she couldn't win."

Moira started, remembering that day twenty years before that she'd broken away from Giulia Pervitto to go and help her brother. Moira had been so young then, and reckless, too. And then the shock upon seeing her brother coming back safely—with Violet.

"She said nothing of the sort," Moira insisted, pushing past her nostalgia. "She could've won and wiped us all out. You wouldn't even have existed. And the world today would be completely Violet Army-ified." She shook her head. "Whatever she was, your mother has changed—completely. You don't have to worry about that, Evolet."

He took a deep breath, and then held it, and then breathed out slowly, and Moira saw some of the heavy serious look disappear from his eyes. She smiled.

"So she isn't a bad guy. She's just Mom," Evolet whispered.

His aunt nodded emphatically. "Yes. She's just your mom now, and she loves you more than you will ever know. It's fine, Evy."

Evolet smiled, and sat up straighter, as if there was a weight taken off his shoulders.

"Just Mom," he breathed. "Good to know. Thanks."

* * *

"This isn't over yet," Conner told Moira over the phone later that evening. "The police have no idea who she was, and blood test results will be back tomorrow. The police chief is keeping in contact with me, since it was Evolet— and us, apparently—that the girl was trying to warn. That alone makes them feel something big is going on."

Moira sighed. "If only people would just stop. Conner... What now?"

"What now?" Conner knew his sister was worried, so he did his best to sound jovial. "Well. We wait. And watch the kids. Is Evolet alright?"

"Yeah, he's asleep—I *think*," Moira added suspiciously. She glanced at the clock across the living room. "And I should be, too."

"Good, so all's well. Should we take the kids to school tomorrow?" Conner wondered aloud.

"You're asking *me?*" Moira returned. "I dunno. Do you think it's safe?"

"Oh, I don't know," Conner sighed. "I think they'll be fine. At least the older three."

"What about Charles? He'll worry," Moira pointed out.

"I guess Vi and I can manage that. It'll work," Conner decided. "And I'm going to talk to their teachers, to keep an eye on them. Nobody is hurting those kids," he added vehemently.

Moira smiled fondly. "Right. Well, I have work tomorrow, so I'll go now. See you, Conner!"

"Goodnight, Moira. See you!" And Conner hung up.

Moira put her phone down to charge, then glanced around the room, yawning. It was quite dark now, and almost eleven at night.

She looked briefly at a picture on the mantel, the one of Evolet as a toddler, and set her jaw firmly. No one was going to be hurting her nephew.

Or her brother or any of the rest of the family, for that matter. But she felt a pang as she realized for the hundredth time in the past few months that

Evolet was more important to her than anyone else.

Quickly, she went around the house, locking all the doors. She did that every night, but tonight she double-checked them. Unusual for Moira, but then again, that day had been unusual. Quite so. And her days were only going to get more unusual. But at this point, that was life.

twenty-eight

Though it was eleven o'clock at night and Moira's bedtime, a couple of states away, the Foleys were having an impromptu meeting. Their three faces were deadly serious, and there was a tense atmosphere in the room, which was only intensified when Petyr stepped in after his two younger siblings and locked the door behind him.

"We all know what happened to Riley Fletcher," he began almost right away, his voice quiet. "Are the three of us going through with this?"

"I still don't get exactly what happened," Jason muttered.

Flynn looked at him in disbelief, and sighed. "Riley went to warn the Whytes. Zaire sent someone after her, and they wiped her out just before she could blurt out the entire thing. The point is, the Whytes are definitely our main target, and if we're on their side—" She drew her finger across her throat meaningfully.

Jason shrugged uneasily. "We have T5 now," he pointed out slowly. "Surely it can't be that dangerous." He glanced down at himself, then at his brother and sister.

They were all somewhat different from a couple of months ago, when they'd gone on the mission to eliminate Louis. All of their eyes were now the same, unnatural coral color that Riley's had been. Jason's hair had been a light brown before, but now it was blond at the roots as well. So was his siblings' hair.

They were dressed in the same style of clothes they usually wore, though Jason and Flynn had had to get new ones a couple of sizes bigger, and there had been some slight changes made to all of the outfits. The dark boots were the same, and the boys' pants, and Flynn's skirt.

There was an embroidered *V* and upside-down *L* on Flynn's and Jason's short-sleeved shirts, and the same emblem on Petyr's jacket—Flynn and Jason's jackets were tied around their waists. But it could be assumed that all the Victor-style tops had the same thing embroidered on them.

"Riley had T5, too," Petyr reminded his brother. "And we have a way to deal with that. In fact, the T5 amplifies the darts we use. It's more dangerous for everyone involved, Jason."

"But..." He fell silent as Petyr's words sunk in.

"Maybe we should forget it," Flynn spoke up suddenly, her eyes downcast. "It's not like Grace is a real relation anymore. She probably doesn't even know we exist."

"But I hate to just murder *kids*," Jason muttered.

Petyr locked eyes with him. "It's us or them. Pick one."

Slowly Jason shook his head. "You can't ask me to do that, Petyr. I can't decide something like that."

"Well, you're going to have to," Petyr returned smoothly, looking at his brother hard. "With Zaire—there is no middle path."

"Jason, it's fine," Flynn told her brother. "They don't know us. We don't know them. They'll have no idea what hit them. But *we* know what's going on, and we have to survive—together. We've been survivors all our lives, we Foleys."

Jason didn't answer her. He turned around, staring out the window at the cow fields.

The field outside the window just happened to be the same one Riley had been walking in weeks before.

Petyr stepped up to him and put his hand gently on his younger brother's shoulder. "Jason, we Foleys work together in everything. You know that. Are you with us and Zaire, or not?"

"Who is Zaire?" Jason wondered softly. His mouth set in a hard, tight line. "We don't even know him."

"Yeah, but he's the boss, and he's calling the shots," Petyr reminded him. "Whoever he is, he has power. And we are some of the highest up. We have power as well. Let's not lose it."

"If you leave, he'll kill you, too, just like Riley," Flynn added. "Don't, Jason."

"Yeah, like Zaire said, it's time for Operation Elimination," Petyr went on, heartened by the fact that Jason wasn't arguing anymore. "Within two weeks, we—I mean the other scientists and I—will have finished the anti-T4 weapon, and we're going to release it over Annapolis. Zaire said we have three weeks before the deadline. We don't have time for anything else, Jason. We're all in it now. For good or for bad. And it's looking good right now."

"How does Tina feel about Riley?" Jason asked suddenly.

"Tina?" Flynn started. "Tina doesn't care."

"I bet she does, really," Jason scowled. "I bet..." Again he broke off, realizing it was impossible.

"You bet what?" Petyr pressed.

Jason shook his head, and turned around. "You guys are right. We have to work together in this."

"You're with us then?" Flynn smiled.

Jason nodded, his face still tight.

"We look out for each other."

* * *

It wasn't just the Foleys who didn't know Zaire—Zaire Keswick. It was everyone except himself—if he even knew himself. Everyone else only knew small hints of the dark thoughts that lay perpetually hidden under that dark—now turning light—hair of his. On most of the outside, he looked like any other average person.

He was probably about fifty, tall, stout, and extremely muscular. But if you looked into his now coral-colored eyes you could catch a glimpse of the evil that was behind them. Perhaps that was why he had a tendency to keep the eye that wasn't covered by a patch, half-closed. No one even knew why he wore the patch. He didn't need it.

He had a scar on his face as well, across his left cheek. Rumor had it that he'd gotten it in a fight with a leopard, somewhere in Africa, which was presumably where he'd come from. And he liked wildcats of that sort. Not many people were allowed into his private office, but the few who were knew that there was a leopard skin on the floor—the leopard skin was reputedly real, acquired by Zaire Keswick himself.

He was pacing in his office at the moment, talking to another man with dark hair and skin—whose hair color was also changing. It was an invariable side effect of the T5, it seemed.

"Tell the scientists to come up with something stronger. Fletcher Junior shouldn't have had time for last words," Zaire complained to the man, who nodded.

"Right, we'll do that." He had a thick accent. "And Liszt?"

"Liszt? Oh, yes." Zaire paused his pacing to glance at a tablet on the desk. There was a report open on the screen. Reading it over again, Zaire nodded.

"She needs to be eliminated, immediately and discreetly. She's too close," he noted decisively.

The man nodded again, and turned to leave.

"Wait," Zaire spoke suddenly, wheeling around to face his subordinate. "There's something else."

"Yes?" the man asked, watching the Victors' leader carefully.

"Have someone watch the Foleys, will you? They're up to something." Zaire's coral eyes narrowed into slits.

Yet another deep nod that was almost a bow. "I will do that, sir."

Zaire watched, a satisfied look coming into his face as the man left, shutting the door behind him. The leader walked over to the desk again, this time to spin a globe that stood there. He watched it turn.

"Soon. Soon it will begin."

twenty-nine

" Hello, this is Conner Whyte, who's this?" Conner asked cautiously into his phone the next afternoon. He wasn't used to getting calls from unknown numbers.

"This is the Annapolis Police Department," came the answer. "Conner Whyte, can you and Violet Whyte come down to the station immediately? It's important."

"Uhh, I think?" Conner ran his hands through his hair in a way like Evolet's—or maybe it was the other way around. "One sec."

He held the phone away from his mouth, and glanced at Violet, who was sitting at the other end of the table, finishing her late lunch.

"Vi," he broke in quickly, and she looked up. "Police station? Prob'ly the test results."

She nodded, still chewing. Conner held his phone to the side of his face again.

"Yeah, we'll be right there. Thanks. See you."

Two seconds later, he hung up, dropping his phone into his pocket. Violet scraped her plate clean and stood up, heading for the sink.

"Give me one minute, and I'll be in the car," she called out, putting the plate in the sink and walking in the direction of her bedroom.

He nodded absently, then seemed to remember something. "You don't have to wear that purple jacket everywhere, you know," he reminded his wife hastily.

Her voice came muffled from down the hall. "It's fine. One of these days I won't wear it, I promise." He could hear her laughing.

Conner smiled to himself, sighing. Violet *would* be violet. But he was glad she left out the potential "n" in that word nowadays.

He went to get his own jacket from the hook by the door and grabbed his keys, easily jumping over and across the front steps down to the driveway. Stepping down them took too long, especially when he was in a hurry. Which he was now.

A few moments later, Violet came bounding down the steps in turn. She lost no time in getting into the passenger seat and buckling herself in.

"Let's go." She grinned confidently.

* * *

"We still have no idea who she was, but that's not why we asked you two to come," the police chief was telling the Whyte couple about half an hour later. "What's relevant right now is that the victim tested positive for T4."

Conner and Violet both started, and Conner blanched visibly. He had not been expecting this, not at all.

"You're kidding," Violet breathed.

The man shook his head glumly. "No, I'm not. But there is one other thing."

"And what's that?" Conner demanded.

"It's... It's not quite the same T4." The police chief hesitated. "There's something different about it. What it is, we don't know. Our scientists are working on it. But this new compound doesn't react to the test strip quite as strongly as the original strain."

"So...a T5?" Violet asked. She closed her purple eyes briefly and then opened them again, staring at Conner to see what his reaction would be when the officer nodded. Which he did.

"So there's something big going on here," Conner surmised, breathing deeply. "Do we know anything else?"

"No. Nothing at all." The officer's face was sober. "So I contacted higher up, and they're working on it. But they wanted me to ask you two to work on it as well. Is that—possible?"

The Whytes glanced at each other.

"We can leave the kids with Moira, I guess," Conner muttered. Violet nodded.

"You're on board, then?" A relieved expression came over the policeman's face.

"Yes," Conner answered for them both.

"Great. Oh, and one more thing." The man turned, and opened a drawer. "We've found out everything we can from this weapon, and we have samples."

He turned to face them again, this time holding a small, sterilized pouch with a dart in it. The small projectile had a V-style feathered end, and a dangerously sharp-looking tip. The officer handed it carefully to Conner.

"Please do not hurt yourself on that," he warned quickly, as Conner lifted it for inspection. "It was tipped with some kind of semi-liquid substance that is absolutely and horrifically lethal to T4—and, I imagine, to T5 as well, if that's what we're calling it. I think my scientists secured a quantity of it to experiment with, but I wouldn't be too sure that it's all gone."

He looked seriously at Conner. "When we applied it to a T4 sample, it burned like fire. Literally. But one of my men accidentally applied it to himself, and he was fine. It's only effective against T4, T5, whatever."

Conner inspected the dart. It looked small and relatively harmless, but he wasn't going to doubt the officer's word that it could kill him.

"Thanks." He managed a weak smile. "For the bad news."

The officer nodded wordlessly. "When can you start tracking?" he asked deferentially a moment later. "So I can make my report."

The two Whytes glanced at each other again.

"Right away," Conner decided. "We'll just stop home for a bit to get what we need and then we can start. Sound good?"

"Perfect," the man assured him. "Thank you."

Five minutes more and Conner and Violet were back in the street. The first thing Conner did was stop walking and stare imploringly at an innocent street sign across the road.

"Oh, joy!" he exclaimed. "What next!"

"Action," Violet returned smoothly, heading across the street towards their car. "And guess what: I'm going to leave my jacket home—we should go incognito. Let's go, Trooper."

He followed her, aghast. "Vi, sometimes you scare me."

She smiled slightly as she took the passenger seat. "Do I really?"

Resignedly, Conner went around to the driver's door, opened it, and sat down, starting the engine. He glanced across the cupholders at Violet.

"Shall we begin?" he asked with affected nonchalance.

Violet arched her eyebrows up. "Well, shall we?"

"That's not a real answer," Conner mumbled, taking the car out of park and guiding it skillfully down the street.

His wife laughed. "You kidding me? Let's do this."

thirty

In the week that passed, Evolet didn't know what his parents were up to, but he could well guess. Jasmine, Alison, and Charles were staying with him and Moira again.

And he knew things were happening. Moira talked to Conner every night, and Evolet's teachers had never watched him so closely before. But there was more than that in the air.

Evolet and Jasmine discussed their little discoveries every day after school, alone, a few rooftops away from Moira's house. Today, Friday, they had something huge to go over. Or Evolet did.

"I'm not kidding, it's real," he was telling his thirteen-year-old younger sister earnestly. "Mr. Rico was talking about it on the phone halfway through class. It really happened."

She shook her head disbelievingly, sitting back slightly on the roof to gaze at the wisps of clouds floating overhead.

"An entire block of former Violet Army prisoners. Alive one night and dead the next morning. How'd they get totaled like that?"

"I don't know," Evolet insisted. "All I know is that it happened."

"Okay, well, that's creepy," Jasmine told him needlessly. "Is this what that girl was talking about, you think?"

"I bet it is." Evolet's voice lowered to a confidential whisper. "I bet that's what Mom and Dad are gone for, too."

She yawned. "We already figured that much."

"Yeah, I know," Evolet shrugged. "Wonder if we'll get to help out this time. Sounds like things are really starting to happen."

"We probably won't," Jasmine muttered pessimistically. "We never do."

"We helped out last time," Evolet reminded her. "But I guess that wasn't quite intentional on your part."

"Of course it was!" Jasmine snorted. "Don't we all know that I saved the day!"

He choked, coughed, and finally managed to laugh. "Mhmm. Right. Of course."

"Anyway," Jasmine ignored him, "we should be looking out for ways to help this time, too. So—"

She broke off as they both saw their aunt step out the door of her house and look around. Evolet mumbled something under his breath.

"Evolet, Jasmine!" Moira yelled a few seconds later. "Dinner!"

"Coming!" the two shouted in unison, and scrambled to beat each other off the roof. Jasmine touched ground half a second after Evolet.

"You're getting to be a pretty good climber," Evolet remarked, semi-proudly.

She tossed her hair. "Better than you," she smirked, breaking into a run while he took the time to raise his eyebrows.

Startled, he tore after her. But she had such a head start that she got to Moira's front porch before he did. Panting, they both grinned at each other before heading inside.

"You shoulda let me win," Evolet gasped. "In fact, we should *both* let each other win sometime."

"Let you win?" Jasmine smiled defiantly. "I only let Charles win. Never people older than me."

"What about Livia?" her brother countered.

Jasmine pulled a face. "Livia's different."

"So are you," he teased, stepping inside and ducking into the restroom to wash his face.

"Hey!"

***

"Everything is all set," Petyr was announcing to Zaire and the others. He gestured towards the diagram of a rocket-style mechanism his scientific colleague had taped up on the wall behind him. "This thing can take out all T4s in Annapolis, no questions asked. Just like in the prison block."

"Discreetly?" Zaire frowned. "The test we did at the prison seems to be all over the news." He glared at one of his subordinates, who instinctively looked very closely at the toes of his shoes.

"Well, yeah, as discreetly as we can get it," Petyr shrugged, somewhat uncomfortably. "People do notice when other people die sometimes— especially when it's genocide. But it's a peaceful death, just falling asleep like that, and as you can see nobody knows exactly what happened in that prison. That is," he corrected himself, "nobody but us."

"Good." Zaire nodded. "That's how it should be. And that's how it's going to be. We all head to Annapolis, for the final setup—tomorrow. Let's all get some rest tonight and be fresh and ready for the move." He looked meaningfully at Petyr, under whose eyes there were shadows of too many late nights.

Petyr smiled slightly. The leader might pretend to care, but Petyr knew he didn't. The scientist had been with the Victors too long.

"Questions?" Zaire asked, but no one had any. "Good. Meeting adjourned. — When this ends, there is going to be a victor, and there is going to be a loser," he intoned, his eyes flitting over every one of his colleagues to make sure they all replied.

"We will be the Victors!" they shouted back.

Every single one of them.

Zaire was satisfied.

* * *

"I'm worried," Violet admitted to Conner later that same evening. "The prison deaths only go to show that we are getting nowhere."

"There are no traces that it was an engineered murder," Conner scowled, shaking his head. "But you're right, everyone with T4... Normal accidents won't kill them. And if that woman had T5, we can assume it's the same people at work here."

"Maybe we should go back to the kids," Violet mused. She managed a half-hearted laugh. "I know you reject this every single time I say it, but what if we went back to Iceland?"

"Vi, we agreed we'd be done running," Conner returned. He paused. "Right?"

"Yes, but we didn't know this was gonna happen," Violet argued, crossing her arms. "*Any* of this. Let alone someone inventing a way to kill us reliably and swiftly."

"We knew there were risks," Conner reminded her softly. "And we can't run forever. Would you really rather we hadn't come back?"

Violet thought for a moment before shaking her head. "No. I can't say I do. I would never know Evolet the way I do now."

"Mhmm," Conner put in thoughtfully. "Evolet's a pretty good kid. Even if I do say so myself," he added, grinning as he guided the vehicle they were in around a corner.

"The poor kids," Violet muttered. "At this point I don't believe their lives will ever be free from...this horrible suspense." She shuddered.

"Vi, I promise," Conner told her earnestly. "Someday, all of this will be over, and our family can be a normal family. I promise." He said it so vehemently she turned to look at him.

"So you *do* care about their leading normal lives," Violet murmured, in an almost querying way.

A helpless look came over his face. "You kidding me? I had a more normal life than you ever did."

"Yeah, something like Evolet's...until we came back." Violet cringed. "Our coming back has changed him so much. I wish he would've decided to stay at our house, but I guess we really can't blame him, after we left him here all these years."

Her face twisted. "I love him so much. I just wish he'd realize that."

"He will," Conner assured her. "He just doesn't know everything you and I went through to give him the bit of normal life he had. I never thought we could do it," he added softly as an afterthought.

And now Violet's face really contorted. "Neither did I." Her voice got quieter and quieter until it almost sounded broken. "And he doesn't know us. Not the way the other kids do. It's almost too much."

"Again, he will, someday," Conner repeated himself. "He can't go through life without realizing what you've done for him."

She smiled faintly. "And what you've done, too. But how long?"

"How long?" Conner echoed. "Who knows? But it'll happen. Meanwhile, we should probably get going," he added as he parked the car. "We're at the prison. Let's investigate!"

Violet laughed warily, pulling a couple of gas masks out of the bag by her feet. "You mean, let's suit up, and *then* investigate." She frowned. "We're not taking any chances with this."

thirty-one

"Everything's ready, Zaire," one of Zaire's dark henchmen reported to him, two days later. "The rocket goes up tomorrow at midnight—well, the day after tomorrow—precisely. Everything is covered. Petyr told me to tell you."

Zaire smiled, an evilly glinting smile. "Perfect. Any updates on the Foleys? Or on Liszt, or on the two Whytes?"

The man shook his head somberly. "No. Foleys seem alright. Liszt has disappeared suddenly—our agents think she's gone to Washington to make her report, which isn't a real report, we hope; the Whytes are still hanging around. But they're in their car most of the time, so we can't get rid of them inconspicuously—yet." He smiled slightly.

Zaire frowned in turn. "Well, keep someone tailing them. They are very likely to get involved once things really get going."

The man bowed. "We will do that."

"Midnight tomorrow..." Zaire mused. "Everyone with the injection knows what to expect, right?"

"I think so," the man returned. "They should."

"Good." Zaire ran through a mental checklist and was delighted to find that there was nothing more to do. "Good, good, good."

He realized the other man was still waiting, watching for a signal. He nodded briefly to him. "You're dismissed."

Bowing again, the man left the room, closing the door behind him. As he did so, Zaire rubbed his hands together excitedly.

"Now it begins, my friends," he murmured to himself. "Now it begins."

* * *

Meanwhile, Jason Foley was in a state of mental agony. He was in a car, alone. He was actually glad to be alone. He couldn't keep his feelings to himself any longer, as was revealed when he finished a can of soda and crushed it slowly in his hands, staring out the dashboard.

He'd been lucky to get away. Flynn and Petyr were worried about him. Well, they were always worried about him, but especially when he was so obviously distracted by some secret that he couldn't remember which car keys were his. But he'd shaken them off his trail. More accurately, they were too busy to look after him at the moment.

The blond tinge in his hair was getting stronger, and his eyes were still that coral color. He had a feeling they were going to stay that way, and he didn't know whether he liked it or not.

But that was only a part of the problem. He was focusing on something entirely different right now as he stared at the small slip of paper in his hands. It was that Whyte kid's phone number. Evolet's.

Jason was thinking of the kids, most especially Evolet and Jasmine. At midnight tomorrow he knew they would be dead. And he'd be twice as strong as they were now. But he didn't care about that. He *did* care about the kids. He didn't want them to die, he knew.

And he had a plan to save them, and the other Whytes. But it would mean turning on his friends and siblings. And there was also a very large chance that it would fail, and he, Jason, would die as well. He still felt he could succeed. But he would need help.

He was very seriously considering calling Evolet on the phone and telling him everything that was going on. He didn't have Conner Whyte's number, but anyway he knew the father was busy. And at this hour, Evolet Whyte should be out of school.

Jason wondered for the millionth time that week if he was even capable of doing this. He was the youngest Foley, and had never been one to take on major operations like this. But he was alone in trying to save the Whytes at this point, he knew.

Could he save them?

They'd definitely be grateful for a complete brief on what was going on, he thought pensively, but even then, Zaire's men might still win.

But if the Whytes and their friends *did* succeed, what then?

He shouldn't care about himself at this point, he knew.

But would they accept him?

And then he remembered Violet. Or Grace. His older sister, the oldest Foley.

He, Jason, knew very little about her, only that she had disappeared about the same time when their parents were murdered. They'd never expected to see her again, and merely assumed she was dead. But she wasn't.

We look out for each other. It was the favorite Foley saying. They counted themselves as survivors—when their parents had died, the eldest left, Petyr, had been five, and Jason had been just a baby. They'd gone from a peaceful home, to a worthless foster house, and now to—the Victors.

"But 'we' and 'each other' includes Grace and her family, right?" Jason asked himself aloud, and jumped. It was startling to hear his own voice.

But he felt Grace would agree. And he figured that even if no one else accepted him, she would have to. She was his sister, after all—and a former terrorist like he was. She would have no excuse not to.

And what of his other siblings? he thought dimly, and suddenly came to a resolve. He would call Evolet. He'd get Conner's phone number from the kid, and then he'd call him too. And then, the next morning, just before putting his plan into action, he would call Petyr and tell him everything. Well, that Jason was defecting. Not the plan, naturally.

Jason managed a weak smile as he reached into his pocket for his phone. It was time to get this started, or he'd be too late. Maybe it was too late already.

But better late than never, right?

thirty-two

As Jason had hoped, Evolet was done with school, though he was doing his homework when his phone rang. He picked it up, glancing at the number. Startled, he stared at it for a moment before answering the call. He didn't recognize the number at all.

"Hello, who's this?" he asked cautiously.

"Evolet Whyte?" came an unfamiliar voice.

"Umm... Yeah, that's my name," Evolet replied, wishing he hadn't answered the call. "Who are you?"

"I'm Jason, Jason Foley. Do you remember me, Evolet?"

"Huh?" Evolet ran his free hand through his hair. "I don't know any Jasons. Or Foleys."

"Okay, well, you know this one." Jason's voice was slightly impatient. "You know Louis Staunton?"

"Oh." Evolet nodded in revelation.

"You remember now?"

"Oh! Yeah, I remember," Evolet affirmed hastily.

"Okay, then, listen up. Are you alone?"

Evolet glanced around his room quickly. "Yeah, I am. What's up? How do you know my phone number?"

"Never mind that now, but I need you to listen, Evolet. There's something big going on, and you guys are right in the middle of it, though you probably don't know that."

Evolet allowed himself a tiny smile, having his suspicions confirmed. "Yeah, well, I guessed that," he returned quickly.

"Okay. So you know Zaire?"

"Who is this Zaire?" Evolet demanded. "The person that stranger talked about, right?"

"You mean Riley Fletcher? Yeah."

"Oh, so *that's* who it was!" Evolet realized. "But she looked different."

"Yeah, so do I. I mean, we all do. But that's not important. Evolet, I need your help."

"Fire away," Evolet told him emphatically, his eyes wide.

"I'll explain tomorrow, but it's a matter of life and death. Can I pick you up during school?"

"Pick me up?" Evolet echoed. "Yeah, I guess. Why?"

"Because, like I said, I need your help. And you can't tell anyone I'm picking you up. No one. You got that?"

"What about my sister?" Evolet wondered.

"I said no one."

"No, I mean, she'll want to help, too," Evolet protested, knowing he would never get away with keeping something like that from Jasmine.

"Which one?" Jason hesitated openly.

"Jasmine," Evolet replied immediately.

"The one Louis kidnapped?"

"Yes." Evolet nodded in spite of the fact that Jason couldn't see him.

Or so he thought. He didn't realize Jason was sitting in the car across the street and looking through the window at his nephew.

"Well, I guess—but no one else. You'll be ready to go during school?"

"Yeah, I'll be ready all day," Evolet assured Jason eagerly.

"Good. If you've got any combat clothes...wear them," Jason told him seriously.

Suddenly an idea struck Evolet. "Hey, how do I know this is the real thing?" he questioned breathlessly. "What if you're just trying to kidnap Jasmine and me so that you can—"

"Use you? Yeah, sure I am. But I really just need to use you temporarily. I need your guys' help. I could very likely get killed for talking to you right now, Evolet, if that means anything to you."

"Who's 'they'?" Evolet wrinkled his brow in confusion.

"Oh, the Victors," Jason told him hurriedly. "I'll explain tomorrow, okay? You can call them the bad guys for short."

"Aha," Evolet laughed. "Okay then."

"But I have to go," Jason went on quickly. "So I will talk to you tomorrow. And don't fail me, 'kay?"

"I won't," Evolet promised him. "Anything else?"

"Not really... Okay, one last thing. I'm your uncle."

"W—what?" Evolet nearly screamed, completely taken by surprise.

"That's exactly it. Text me your dad's number, okay? ASAP?"

"Okay, but—"

"Got to go. I'll talk to you tomorrow!"

"See you, but—"

Evolet stopped talking as he heard the dial tone. Jason had hung up on him.

He stared at his phone in a state of semi-shock for a moment, then jumped up, texting Conner's phone number to Jason quickly and then shoving his phone into his pocket.

He glanced out the window, not realizing that Jason—his uncle, apparently—was driving away. But Evolet did realize that it was almost dark, and that he had to hurry if he wanted to talk to Jasmine. Grabbing his coat, he pulled it on and headed out into the hallway.

"Jaz. Jasmine!" he yelled for his sister.

A moment later she poked her head out Moira's bedroom door. "'Sup?"

"Let's go outside quickly, before it's too dark," Evolet blurted out, his purple eyes meeting her blue ones.

She nodded, taking in the deadly serious look in his eyes. "Okay. Aunt Moira, I'm going out with Evolet!"

"It's dark," Moira put in from the kitchen.

"Y—e—a—h, I guess, but not too dark, right?" Evolet pleaded desperately. "Just five minutes? Please?"

"Fine," Moira acquiesced. "But I'm setting a timer. And bring your phone."

"Got it," Evolet replied, leaping into the air jubilantly, then turning to leave.

Jasmine caught up with him as he opened the door, and she grabbed his arm. "Evy, what's going on?" she whispered, with the air of a fellow conspirator.

"Shh, tell you on the roof," he murmured back, slamming the door shut behind the two of them and breaking into a run. He beat her that time, in the race and in the climbing too. Panting, Jasmine pulled herself up next to him, and glared.

"I let you win," she declared vehemently, smirking.

"Mhmm, yeah, right," Evolet replied as a matter of course, but he was distracted. "Jaz, I just got a call from that Jason person. You remember the five strangers that helped us beat Louis? Well, he's one of them, and I guess he is turning to our side," he told her, talking so fast he could barely understand himself. "He's gonna pick you and me up during school tomorrow and we have to be dressed for a fight. And we can't tell Aunt Moira, and—"

"Stop, stop, stop." Jasmine held up her hands as if they could stop the torrent of information. "Jason who?"

"Jason Foley. He said he's my—our—uncle—"

"What? We haven't *got* any uncles," Jasmine muttered.

Evolet threw his hands in the air. "I don't know, Jasmine, just listen!" he shouted.

She turned, and stared at him. "Okay," she answered finally, toning down the ordinary grin on her face to a serious frown. "I'm listening."

"He needs our help to, uhh, not let the Victors kill us," Evolet began, more slowly this time. "I mean, he needs my help, but he agreed that I could tell you—"

"Hey, you'd have to tell me anyway," Jasmine interrupted, tossing her hair.

Evolet felt like he was going to scream. "Jaz, just *shut up!*"

He was somewhat surprised, but nonetheless gratified, to get a sort of shocked silence from the younger teen. She sighed resignedly, watching him closely.

"So, we should dress specially for fighting tomorrow," Evolet went on. "He's going to tell us the plan once he picks us up." He stopped.

"Is that all?" Jasmine asked, with a sarcastically timid air.

Evolet closed his eyes, remembering. "I think... Oh, yeah, he said it's a matter of life and death, and we can't tell anyone. I guess that includes Aunt Moira."

"But we have to tell her," Jasmine protested. "If she asks us, I mean."

"Right, so be super good so that she *won't* ask us," Evolet smirked. "Got it?"

Jasmine laughed. "Okay, got it. What time is it?"

"Time to head inside, I guess," Evolet muttered. "Anyway. Don't say a word about it. Just don't forget in the morning—oh, what should we wear?"

"I've got my...umm...fighting suit thingy that Mom designed me," Jasmine remembered. "Oh, but you..."

"Don't have one," Evolet finished dully.

Jasmine shut her eyes, and then opened them suddenly as her hand shot up towards the sky. "I've got it! You can wear Mom's!"

"What?" Evolet stared in frank astonishment at the proposal. "You're kidding?"

"No, you're about as tall as Mom, and anyway she left her jacket and night vision goggles at home," Jasmine explained, grinning. "And her boots, I think. So you can borrow 'em."

"You think?" Evolet asked, brightening up hopefully. "You think she'd let me?"

"Well, yeah, and anyway—" Jasmine began, but then the door to the Whyte house opened.

"Evolet! Jasmine!" Moira shouted.

"We're coming!" Evolet yelled back, and swung himself to the edge of the roof. He paused momentarily, and glanced at Jasmine.

"And anyway, what?" he asked quickly.

Jasmine grinned, hanging off the roof and then dropping. "And anyway, well, ask me tomorrow and I'll show you where Mom's stuff is!"

* * *

"What do you mean, *wait!*" Violet shrieked at Conner, once he got off the phone with Jason. "If they're going to do what that man said they are, then we need to stop them *now!*"

"Vi, you don't get it," Conner broke in hurriedly. "He's risking his life to help us, and he knows what we're all up against. We have to trust him and not do anything about it till tomorrow. And we have to trust him that there are assassins after us, and we have to stay careful." He spoke seriously.

"I can't believe this," Violet fumed. "Death is hanging over us by a thread, and you're telling me to *wait!*"

"I can't help it, Vi," Conner returned, somehow managing to keep his voice quiet. "We have to. Okay?"

"Okay, I guess," Violet mumbled, in an exceedingly bad temper. Finally she looked up, and sighed. "So what did he say for us to do, exactly? And when do we do it?"

thirty-three

That night was a peaceful one in Annapolis. No one would have ever guessed that it could well be the last night of an entire family's lives, and that most of the family knew it.

Evolet didn't know how he got to sleep, but he did. So did Jasmine. But they both looked tired the next morning, which was to be expected, since they were so excited they set their alarm clocks for five-thirty in the morning.

They met in the hall ten minutes after that, their faces washed, their teeth brushed, and their morning prayers said, though the teenagers themselves were still in pajamas. The two siblings glanced at each other seriously for a moment, and Jasmine gestured to her older brother to keep silent as she turned and led the way towards the room their parents used when they stayed over.

"Mom's suitcase is in here," she whispered to Evolet as he closed the door. He nodded wordlessly, looking around.

The room was just like any normal bedroom, but there was a smallish, compact-style teal suitcase lying open on the bed. The two tiptoed over to it, as if they were afraid there was someone else in the room whom they would wake up if they moved too loudly, though the nearest other human beings were fast asleep in their beds down the hall.

"Right," Jasmine breathed as she pushed aside the top layer of clothes. "Here we go."

She pulled out the light purple jacket of unidentifiable material, with a Violet Army symbol faintly etched near the left shoulder, and held it up to Evolet, grinning. It looked like it was going to fit him perfectly.

He let out a small outrush of air, then glanced at Jasmine as next she pulled out a pair of long, rubber, dark purple boots, a pair of goggles, and a belt with a holster.

Evolet suddenly realized he wasn't wearing his day clothes yet. Taking off the jacket, he put everything in his arms to carry back to his room. Jasmine was already sneaking out.

There was a scrap of purple sticking out from underneath the other clothes, purple the same color as his mom's jacket, and Evolet tugged at it.

He was stunned to discover a baby-sized purple jacket, exactly the same model as his mother's, but definitely much smaller. It looked like it had been handmade, though. And as he inspected it, he found an inscription, painstakingly embroidered on the back of the collar:

Little Trooper.

Evolet stared at it, stunned. He had no memory of this, but he did have a dim sense of having seen it before. It was an ethereal feeling.

And then there was a memory of warmth. A hug. A light, butterfly kiss on the forehead.

Someone's laugh, and the word, "Evolet."

"*Mom?*" he whispered in shock.

"What?" Jasmine asked from the doorway, and he looked up and realized she was staring at him in confusion.

Evolet jumped. "Nothing, I—" He paused, holding up the jacket. "Was this Charles's?"

Jasmine wrinkled her brow. "Nah, it wasn't. I've never seen it before. Where'd you find it?" she asked him curiously, going back over to the bed.

He let her take it out of his hands, still feeling numb in shock. "I—it was just in there."

She looked at him, then it, then him again, and dropped the jacket onto the suitcase's other contents.

"Evy, I have no idea. You can ask Mom later, I guess. But let's go now, 'kay? Today isn't PJ day at school, silly!"

He managed a laugh before following her down the hall. But as he got dressed and then put on his mother's jacket, belt, and boots, setting the holster aside and stuffing the goggles into the jacket pocket, he couldn't stop thinking about the brief memory.

He was sure the laugh and the voice were Violet's. But...

"Mom," he whispered again, and smiled to himself, wishing Violet was there as he remembered Moira's words the other evening.

"She's just your mom now, and she loves you more than you will ever know."

"I think I might know a bit more now," he mused, zipping up the jacket halfway.

Jasmine tapped on the door. Checking that the jacket pockets were zipped up, Evolet hurried over.

"Shh!" he warned. "Do you want to wake up Charles?"

She shrugged. "Come on, let's go on a warm-up run!"

* * *

A few hours later, Jason parked his small car in front of the Annapolis high school building. He glanced up at it momentarily, wondering why it was so quiet before realizing that all of the children were probably in classes. As they should be.

He sighed, wistfully reminiscent of the days he'd done the same thing. His older siblings hadn't had as much of an opportunity for that, especially not Petyr—it was Zaire who picked the three up out of the gutters. So Jason had gotten most of the benefit of a regular schooling.

Having finished scoping out the school, Jason picked up his phone from his lap, took a deep breath, closed his eyes, and then opened them again and dialed his older brother's number. He knew Flynn would only try to convince him not to do it. But he could trust Petyr not to get emotional—well, not to get as emotional as a girl would, anyway.

"Jason, what's up?" his brother asked him, answering the phone. "You're getting the explosives, right? Hey, what's taking so long?"

Jason allowed himself a longish pause, long enough for him to glance at a box on the back seat. A box that was filled with explosives, intended to be used to destroy the evidence of the Schwann2—the rocket machine that would release the anti-T4 toxin into the sky over Annapolis.

"Yeah, I've got 'em. Petyr?"

"Yeah?" came his brother's voice.

"There's something you need to know." Jason paused again. "Petyr, I'm not going along with this. I just had to let you know. I'm outta this, 'kay?"

He thought he heard a strangled gasp from the other end of the call.

Or maybe he actually did.

"Jason!" Petyr managed.

Jason shut his eyes again. "So this is goodbye, Petyr. Tell Flynn for me, okay?"

"Jason, why are you doing this—"

"This is goodbye, Petyr," Jason told his older brother again, quietly and simply. And without waiting for another reaction, he hung up.

And threw his phone out the open car window, shattering it beyond repair.

That done, he grabbed a pair of shaded glasses to conceal his coral-colored eyes. Pulling his hat low over his face, he got out of the car, grabbed his keys, and headed into the school building.

thirty-four

Evolet had long been expecting the classroom door to open in the middle of class, and a stranger to peer in and ask for Evolet Whyte, but he was somewhat surprised nevertheless when it actually did happen. The boy was surprised, because at this point—almost noon—he was nearly ready to simply assume it had been a prank call. But the stranger looked real enough, despite the hat and tinted glasses.

"Hey, is Evolet Whyte in this class?" Jason asked the teacher timidly, though he was already looking over the students. He saw Evolet at the same time as the fifteen-year-old's hand crept up into the air.

"Oh. There he is." Jason nodded to the teenager, and Evolet stood up.

The teacher looked perplexed. "Yes, there's Evolet. But—may I ask what's going on?" he added as Evolet started walking over to the classroom doorway, leaving everything on his desk.

Evolet paused, looked at his teacher in surprise, then at the stranger—and back at the teacher. "I—I have an appointment, right, Uncle Jason?" he asked, blinking confusedly.

"Uhh, yeah, yes you do, actually," Jason stammered, catching on just in time.

But the poor teacher looked befuddled. "...Okay then," he mumbled finally, adding something else under his breath as the two left the classroom and made their way out of the building.

"Where's your sister?" Jason asked Evolet hurriedly, glancing over to the car and looking relieved that nothing had happened to it. "Can you get her? And I mean quickly? We have to be on our way by noon."

Evolet checked his watch: it was seven minutes to the hour. "Yeah, I'll get her," he assured Jason. "Hold on a sec." With that, he dashed off in the direction of the other school building.

It took him fifteen seconds to get there, and fifteen more to get up the steps, into the building, and to the doorway of his younger sisters' classroom. The hallway was empty.

Sliding up against the door, Evolet waved to Jasmine, who'd apparently been waiting for the signal as avidly as him. She stood up, and through the door Evolet heard her asking the teacher if she could go to the bathroom.

Jasmine's teacher, a sharp young woman, said yes, and a few seconds later Jasmine joined her older brother in the corridor.

"Meet you outside," she breathed. "Sixty seconds and no longer."

"You have thirty," he muttered, but as she took off for the restroom he had no choice but to head back outside. True to her word, Jasmine met him there—less than a minute later.

"You're going to have to call my teacher and tell her an emergency came up," she gasped to Evolet as they bolted together towards Jason's car. "So this Uncle Jason person is real?"

"You bet he is," Evolet returned, pointing ahead of them.

Jasmine looked over him as they approached. "Looks like a creep," she muttered to herself—a judgment that was only confirmed when Jason whipped off his hat and glasses to reveal coral eyes and blond-to-brown hair.

Evolet held up both hands, a smirk coming over his face. "Now, wait a sec. I know you're in a hurry, but before we hop in that car you have to prove you're... 'fair dinkum,' as my Australian friend would say. My sister and I know there's something going on, but that doesn't mean you're on our side, see? And you look a lot like that...Riley Fletcher person. So—"

"Yeah, I can prove it," Jason broke in. "Look. Did you hear about T5?"

"T5?" Jasmine stared. "Whazzat?"

"It's like what you kids have, but not as strong. It does this to you," Jason went on, gesturing up towards his eyes and hair. He glanced hard at Jasmine. "We made it using your blood."

Jasmine took a step back. "Whoa, what—"

"Prove it," Evolet told Jason steadily. "And prove that you're on our side."

Hesitating only a moment, Jason stepped forward, and grasped his nephew's hand, holding it tightly. Evolet didn't flinch, but gripped back, just as tightly—and tighter.

Jason smiled. "Convinced?"

Evolet laughed recklessly. "Not yet."

With that, he suddenly twisted his arm around, catching Jason off guard. He flipped around so that their arms were together, and then he started pushing Jason down. The man stared questioningly.

"Fight back," Evolet told him, still grinning. "You can't hurt me."

Jason looked hard at the teenager.

"Okay then," he grunted.

With a sudden move, he flipped Evolet off his feet and onto the ground. He expected it to be over then, but with amazing agility Evolet grabbed his arm before he could fall, and yanked himself back up, swinging his other arm at Jason's chin. Jason dodged the blow, realizing that the teenager was really serious about fighting and that Jason would have to actually fight back if he wanted to prove he had T5 in his blood.

"You can't hurt me!" Evolet yelled at him, watching him carefully. Jasmine stood a few feet away, looking at them anxiously.

Jason reacted by kicking him off his feet again. But this time, when Evolet caught his arm, he was ready for it. He held onto the boy's arm and punched him in the face, though not quite as hard as he could have.

Evolet ignored the pain and swung his hard-booted foot, just grazing the man's chin. Jason retaliated with a hard knock to the boy's stomach, realizing he was running out of time.

Before Evolet recovered from his first stomach blow from a T5-ified antagonist, Jason shoved him again, hard, and Evolet just managed to save himself by grabbing hold of a lamp post and swinging around it.

He stared up at his uncle, a new and honest look of respect in his purple eyes. "Okay. I believe you now," he gasped out.

Jason smiled cautiously. "You okay?" he asked, rubbing his own chin ruefully.

"Y—yeah, I'm okay," Evolet decided, letting go of the post and standing up straight, though he still seemed somewhat out of breath. "But you *can* pack a punch. What's next?"

"I'm from the streets," Jason admitted, grinning for a moment before growing serious. "Okay, I dunno what you guys were planning next, but we have to get out of here," he explained hurriedly. "It's been about five minutes now since I called my brother, and we can't stick around—in case Zaire's men find out what I'm doing now.

"I know my brother—now that he knows what I'm doing, he's going to keep it quiet as long as possible—but we still shouldn't be here. And it's noon," Jason added, checking his watch, "which means you kids have exactly twelve hours left to live, unless we get started, and fast."

Evolet nodded gravely, somewhat too winded from his first loss to make further protest. Jasmine walked over quickly as Jason led the way towards his car.

"Wait—there's someone in there," Jasmine pointed suddenly, and Jason stopped short, and stared at his car.

She was right. Someone was sitting in the back seat, and Jason remembered suddenly that he'd forgotten to lock the vehicle.

Leaping the distance to the car in two bounds—it took Evolet and Jasmine one—he flung the door open, only to find a terrified-looking girl about Jasmine's age sitting there in the back seat. She'd been looking into the explosives box, but as the door was opened suddenly she glanced up and gave a little scream.

"What are you doing here?" Jason demanded, getting over the momentary panic but still sounding a bit harsh. "What's your name?"

"Li—Livia Parson," the girl whispered, staring at him in shock.

"Oh, it's Livia!" Jasmine exclaimed. "Hey, Jason, she's fine. She's my BFF."

"But she's—" Jason began, and gave up a moment later as Jasmine scrambled into the car and sat down next to her best friend.

"Livia, what're you doing here?" she demanded of the younger girl avidly.

"I been watching you," Livia smirked. "You were up to something, I knew. So I decided to follow. What's up? Want any help?"

"I really don't think so," Evolet began, but Jason had been thinking carefully.

"Hey, wait," he broke in, and the three children glanced at him in surprise. He cleared his throat slightly. "Livia, do you have T4?"

"T4? What on earth?" she exploded.

"No, she doesn't, and she doesn't know about it either," Jasmine told Jason quickly.

He nodded, an idea forming in his mind. "Okay. Livia, how about you come with us? We could use your help."

"Huh?" Livia blinked. "I—I was just—"

"Yeah, come!" Jasmine shouted enthusiastically—and covered her mouth self-consciously as Evolet glared her into silence.

"If you don't have T4, some of the Victors' weapons will be ineffective against you," Jason continued, ignoring the fact that the girl had no idea what he was talking about. "So can we kidnap you temporarily? I can call your parents. Wait, no, I can't, my phone is out of commission—"

"I can," Evolet volunteered generously. "I have to call Jaz's teacher anyway."

"You can?" Jason blinked. "Okay, then, cool. Everyone, hop in. We have to get going!"

* * *

Despite Jason's words about no time to lose, the school day was over before things really got going. Jason, Evolet, Jasmine, and Livia had discovered that their car was being tailed, and so Jason ended up taking the kids out-of-state. But at that point, no one was following them anymore, and Jason assured them they would get back in time. Even if it was almost three o'clock PM already.

The kids had put on Victor uniforms Jason had brought with him, and also packed backpacks with gas masks, gloves, and the like, though Evolet insisted on wearing his mother's jacket, especially when Jasmine pointed out that it was bullet-proof.

So they'd moved on to the planning part of the agenda—most of which they'd already done in the car. It was a good thing they'd had an hour to do that, because it took Livia most of that time to even start figuring out what was going on, at which point Jason, Jasmine, and Evolet were thoroughly unamused.

Finally, Livia got a grasp on the situation, even if "none of it made any sense," and now Jason was explaining what they needed her help for, on the way back to Annapolis—in a rental car.

"You guys should probably take a nap on the way back. We're going to be up late. Or you can eat an early dinner. I dunno." Jason was definitely flustered with having to take care of three children, being a youngest himself with no thoughts at all of getting married.

"But, Livia, I'm going to drop you off at the Whytes' house, okay? Can you get...what's her name...Moira Whyte? To help you out? I mean, I dunno what you'd do, but maybe you can just go home and Moira can help. Because the Victors' weapons they'll be using won't affect either of you."

Livia tossed her hair. "Me go home? You kidding? After you just told me this crazy story which makes no sense—except it does—"

"Yeah, your parents will want you home," Jason interrupted, changing his route to head for a train station. "But can you stop at the Whytes'?"

thirty-five

Luckily for Livia, Moira knew much more about the situation than the thirteen-year-old did, and so when Livia was dropped off it only took a few minutes of explaining for Moira to comprehend the situation.

"Can't people at least ask before they borrow my nieces and nephews?" she grumbled, heading outside to the car—it was about time to pick up the kids, after all, even if "the kids" were only Alison and Charles at this point. "Really, the nerve! And—"

"Sorry, but what should I do?" Livia interrupted, timidly and politely.

Moira glanced at her. "You're joking, right? You should get home. Immediately. Or I can bring you to school and your parents can pick you up there. They'll probably be worried stiff," she mused, "just like I would've been if Evolet and Jasmine showed up. Right? Right. So in you go," she finished, opening the side door for the younger girl.

Livia was much disappointed, and somewhat annoyed, after all the trouble she'd taken to be in on the action. But there was no arguing with a stressed, unfamiliar adult, so the girl decided to give up. For the time being.

Nevertheless, it was Moira, and only Moira, who ended up approaching the Victors' base—she had called Evolet, who'd had given her the address—alone, around eleven PM. She had left Alison, Charles, and Livia at Livia's home and asked her parents—politely but urgently—to watch them carefully. And then Moira was free to do her work.

She knew that Jason, Jasmine, and Evolet were already in the building—she had been talking to Jason on the phone—and that they expected her to park her car nearby the large structure and call the police once the signal was given.

So she parked her car and waited. But while she waited, she looked over the building. Jason had called it the "Base."

It was huge, actually, even though it was only one story high—she could bet that there were other underground levels, though. The walls outside were literally plastered with warnings that this was a chemical laboratory—that no one was to tamper with the property.

It was a fit label for this place, Moira thought ironically to herself; definitely better than the Violet Army's old gun shop cover. No one would suspect a chemical laboratory of being anything else. And it *wasn't* anything else, according to Jason.

Moira wasn't happy to see two darkly dressed strangers come marching militarily out of the Base and towards her car, about ten minutes after she'd parked. She glanced at the men, taking in the *V* and upside-down *L* embroidered on their stiff-looking uniforms. Understandably, she was rather doubtful about rolling down the window to talk to them, but when they marched directly up to her car and motioned for her to do so, she realized that she'd better comply or she would give the entire thing away. Which was exactly what Jason had warned her against. So she rolled down the glass, her free hand discreetly on her hidden gun.

"People aren't supposed to hang around this lab—it's dangerous," one of the men told her curtly. "Do you have anything to do here?"

Moira nodded emphatically. "Yeah, I've got business here," she explained, not one bit less curtly. "With the boss. Is he in?"

The other guard gave her a hard scrutiny before nodding. "Yes. He should be."

"Cool. I'm going to pay him a visit," Moira decided, opening her car door completely and stepping out slowly—her hand still in her pocket. With the gun.

They nodded, and backed a few feet away to allow her to walk first towards the laboratory doors. Moira sensed their eyes on her as she reluctantly put her hand on the doorknob, and turned it resignedly, her mind racing. Jason hadn't warned her about this.

She stepped into the building hesitantly.

The next instant, she felt a sharp sting in her elbow, and wheeled around to see one of the guards lowering a kind of gun she didn't recognize. They were watching her.

After the first moment of nearly having a heart attack, Moira leaned against the door frame, glancing down at her elbow. It was a V-feathered dart—just like the one that had been used to kill the woman who'd tried warning Evolet. Riley Fletcher, Jason had told her.

Another thing Jason had told Moira was that the darts would be useless against her. Repressing a smile, the woman tightened her fingers around the handle of her own gun.

With swift, fluid movements that revealed the active girl she had once been, and still was, she stood up straight again, pulling the gun out of her pocket.

The two guards stared at her in shock and horror, and one of them lifted his dart gun to shoot again, but Moira shook her head, finally letting herself smile.

"Okay, this does hurt—slightly—but I don't think that's the reaction you were expecting, am I right?" she told them. "Anyway. Turn around," she ordered, "and get into my car. Now. Oh, and please put your guns down. All of them."

They looked slightly hesitant, but they weren't about to risk getting shot, and so they finally complied, dropping their dart-throwers as well as two real guns that they had with them. Turning around, they walked towards the car quickly, hoping Moira wouldn't change her mind and decide to shoot them with their own darts.

"Get in," Moira called from behind them, "and close the doors. Now."

Which was what they did.

Still smiling, Moira pulled her car keys out of her pocket and hit a button. It was gratifying to see the startled look on one of the guards' faces as he tried the door and found it wouldn't unlock.

"Child safety lock!" She grinned and turned around, picking up the weapons they'd so kindly left for her. "And T4-proof windows," she added under her breath. Evolet had checked those for her.

In the car behind her, one of the guards prepared to smash the window, but his companion held up a hand. "Wait," he whispered, "wait til she goes inside."

The first one looked at him in surprise. "What?" he demanded impatiently.

Chuckling softly, the man gestured towards the door. It was the one on the side away from the building.

"It's not closed," he explained briefly. "It'll open. Just let her go inside first. And then we can warn Zaire."

thirty-six

Inside the Base, however, Jason, Evolet, and Jasmine were already running into trouble. It started when someone they brushed by in the hallway remarked casually that Jasmine was rather short. He stopped to stare—too long—and realized that the two shorter ones, one with purple eyes and one with blue, were most certainly not Victors.

The soldier may have changed his mind about that when the three proceeded to beat him up thoroughly, teaching him a lesson which culminated in Jasmine's shoving him into a closet, with the parting remark that her mom always said Jasmine was going to be even taller than her. But it was too late, and the damage was done, as Jason and his companions realized a few seconds later when the hallway flooded with Victors.

The three fought together quite well, but the numbers were against them, and someone recognized Jason and radioed Zaire. Jason yelled for them to split up. He would contact Conner and Violet—who should have already been there—and the two teenagers would take out the power. He'd given them a verbal layout of the entire Base, so they should know how to find the power room—if they remembered.

"Okay!" Evolet and Jasmine yelled back at the top of their lungs.

They broke away from the Victors they were fighting with at the time, exhilarated to find that they were still stronger than everyone else around them, and that the Victors weren't using darts. The room was so tight that if they started to use those they'd massacre their own friends.

Jasmine darted down a hallway, quickly managing to lose the first wave of pursuit. Taking in her surroundings carefully, she deduced that she was going the right way.

It took her about ten minutes to find her destination, incapacitate the two Victors she encountered, and lock herself in the power room. She glanced around, looking at all the circuit breakers arranged along the walls.

Taking a deep breath as her pulse raced, she leapt over to the first set, and started flipping the switches. It was time to get this over and done with.

* * *

Zaire was infuriated to be informed of the situation and of Jason's betrayal. He paced in his temporary office—a private room in the Base—and muttered in his native language as his subordinate blurted out everything that was going on.

"... And our scouts say the Whyte couple is on the way, and two guards just got back in from being attacked by Moira Whyte," the man reported breathlessly. "Oh, and Petyr Foley says the rocket is leaking—"

"Shut up!" Zaire roared, suddenly losing his patience, and the man did just that. "Okay. First, tell everyone to eliminate all intruders immediately, and at all costs. Secondly, send Petyr and Flynn Foley to the rocket. I don't care if it's leaking, though—in fact, that's good for us, so keep it that way. Make sure the timer keeps going—and switch it to the backup generator.

"I want Conner and Violet to meet with no serious opposition at first—let them get inside the building before you wipe them out. We can't let them escape. If you can't kill them, just keep them around till midnight—that should do it. Moira Whyte is here, too, you said? I don't care about her. Shoot her!"

"O—okay," the man stammered. "Okay." He watched Zaire fearfully.

"What are you waiting for?" the African demanded finally. "Go!"

As the man ducked out, bowing apologetically, Zaire slammed his fist on his desk. Without seeming to realize that it hurt, he picked up his own gun and left the room after his subordinate, a purposeful gleam coming into his coral eyes. He knew exactly what to do.

* * *

"Here's the place," Conner announced needlessly as he parked the truck he and Violet were using across the street from the chemical laboratory. "Hey, that's Moira's car, isn't it," he realized as he and Violet reached for their helmets. "Wonder what she's doing here? But the car is empty."

"'Xpect we'll find her inside," Violet returned, her voice getting muffled halfway through the sentence. "Come on, we're late."

They were wearing old Violet Army battle suits, taken out of storage where they'd sat unused for the last twenty years. They'd figured they'd need them on a mission like this—the first really dangerous mission of their lives, Violet had remarked sarcastically. But she really meant it. In 2024, there had been no way to kill T4-injected people instantly.

"But Moira isn't supposed to be inside," Conner realized as he and Violet made their way to the innocent-looking front laboratory doors. "She's supposed to be waiting for the signal, so she can call the police." He stopped in the middle of the road, and glanced back at the empty vehicle.

"Oh, for heaven's sake, Conner!" Violet grabbed his arm and jerked him out of the path of an incoming car. "Your sister is older than you; she can take care of herself, just like we can. Can't you see where you are? Let's go!"

"Can't see in this thing at all," he muttered, letting her pull him towards the doors. "Your fault, too."

"I wasn't the Violet Army uniform designer," she returned breezily, though she glanced at him with a momentary look of anxiety. "What, is it fogging up?"

"Mhmm," Conner mumbled. He hit the side of his helmet, and a light came on. Now he could see—sort of.

"Why does it fog up?" Violet sighed. "Mine doesn't do that. Never did."

"We can figure that out later—"

"We had twenty years to figure it out—"

"Yeah, but we weren't planning on using these things again!" Conner gritted. "Okay, let's go."

He ran the last few yards to the doors, taking a moment to peer inside before he jerked one of the doors open. The front room was, surprisingly, empty—but the next door wasn't locked, and he held it open for Violet to go in first, a smirk on his face.

She shook her head. "Nah, you first. You're my bodyguard, remember?" she asked playfully.

He nodded seriously. "Right, Trin!"

"Okay, never mind." Violet pulled a face and stepped into the room regardless of what she'd said. "There's no one in here anyway. Why not? Where'd they go?" she questioned the empty room.

"Search me," Conner shrugged, following her in and closing the door behind them both. "But Jason said to cause a disturbance. How do we do that?"

"Like this I suppose," Violet suggested, already heading for the door at the other end of the room. "Let's just waltz in. I mean, seriously. They can't do anything to us in these suits."

"Still seems too easy," Conner muttered, but he followed her anyway as he pulled out his phone. "Since Moira isn't out there, I'd better call the cops now before things get too warm."

"Good idea," Violet called over her shoulder. "But this hallway is empty, too."

Conner was still waiting for the call to go through. "Hold on, wait for me!"

* * *

Somewhere else inside the Base, Zaire was waiting for the alarm—it went off when Conner and Violet crossed the threshold. As soon as it sounded, he motioned to an expectant Victor, who came over quickly and nodded, ready for orders.

"Once they get into Hall B2, blockade the front doors. No one else is getting in—or out—until we've wrapped things up here, for good."

thirty-seven

While Jasmine was confidently making her way towards the power room to put out the electricity, Evolet was completely lost. He felt that he was going in circles—and then the lights went out suddenly, without warning.

He didn't use his phone as a flashlight, because his battery was already extremely low from repeated attempts to call Jason, Violet, and Conner in the last ten minutes. He stopped walking, waiting for his eyes to adjust to the darkness; then he remembered the supposedly night-vision goggles in his jacket pockets. Well, his mom's jacket pockets.

The fifteen-year-old unzipped the pocket with the goggles carefully, pulling them out. He froze as he thought he heard something drop on the floor; but was there anything to drop? Quickly, he fitted the goggles over his eyes. They didn't help.

Desperately, he ran his hands around the edges and across the band. Surely there had to be some way to activate them. Unless they were just too old?

But finally he seemed to press something, and suddenly he could see quite clearly. It was a faint, purple-tinted view, but much better than just blackness. Heartened by that, he continued experimenting, and discovered powerful built-in flashlights. With those on, he looked around to try and see what he'd dropped. Or maybe he had just imagined the sound, because he couldn't see anything.

Shrugging, he put his hand into his pocket to make sure there was nothing in it—and for the first time, he realized there *was* something in it. Or rather, two things. He pulled them out, holding them in the light where he could see them, and stared in surprise at two purple vials.

He caught his breath, trying to wonder what they could be, but he already knew what they were. They had to be T4.

Evolet shook his head dizzily, telling himself it had to be something else. T4 wasn't supposed to exist in vials like these anymore, except maybe in some top-secret government laboratories. There was no way these things were T4.

But it was his mother's jacket... And his mother had been...

No. He shook the thoughts away firmly.

Moira had told him that Violet was good now, and Evolet was going to believe that. No matter what happened.

Setting his jaw firmly in resolve, he replaced the vials in the pocket and zipped it up. He could ask his mom about it later. She would have an explanation. And maybe they weren't even T4. Most definitely they were something else. They had to be.

Evolet began marching forward purposefully, determined to finally find a way out of this maze of dark hallways and dead ends. But he only got as far as the end of that particular hallway when he heard a noise behind him. His heart skipped a beat as he swung around, his spine tingling. Someone else was there.

He took in the scene instantly through the goggles. There was a man there, some feet behind him. He'd been bending down to pick something up off the floor, but now he stood, watching Evolet. They stood like that for only a second at most, but it seemed like much longer. Evolet noted the thick black hair that was light blond at the roots, the eyes that came through the purple-tinted goggles unnaturally, the dark Victor suit, the weapon at the man's side, the scar on his face, the strong and menacing build.

In turn, the man found Evolet to be a tall boy in Victor uniform, with non-Victor goggles on his face, and a surprised expression on his face that showed he knew he was not supposed to be here. Purple eyes—or was that the goggles? The man couldn't tell. But the boy's hair was very definitely dark brown, and the man tensed.

"Who are you?" the man demanded of him, the first to speak.

Evolet stared back unblinkingly, the thought racing through his mind that he simply didn't want to blurt out his real name.

"Trooper A2," he replied on the inspiration of the moment.

The man shook his head. "No. There is no Trooper A2. There only ever was one Trooper. But he's—"

"No, there are a lot more of us than you think there are," Evolet interrupted quickly, his pulse racing. "And we're hard to kill. But who are you?"

"Who am I?" Zaire echoed; and as he had been the first to speak, he was also the first to smile. A smile that instinctively gave Evolet some kind of queasy feeling. "No, you don't need to know who I am. But I think I know who *you* are. And I have a strong suspicion that you don't belong here, young Whyte."

"Don't belong here?" Evolet repeated, breathing slowly and deeply to steady his nerves. "You're the one who's trying to kill us." He figured Zaire would recognize him, if Jason and the others had. "So yeah, I think I belong here."

Zaire shrugged. "Have it your way."

Already tense, he braced himself for a pounce—and stopped suddenly, just as Evolet was ready to sidestep him. Zaire had his own way of fighting. He'd tested it on wildcats in Africa.

True to his custom, he waited for Evolet to attack him, and then he lunged to the right suddenly, kicking the boy's legs out from underneath him.

Not expecting that move, Evolet lost his balance for a moment, but then regained it—just in time to catch Zaire's solid punch to the jaw. Evolet stepped back, seemingly daunted, but suddenly he dropped to the ground in a ball and rolled straight at Zaire.

Zaire kicked at him, but Evolet grabbed his leg and twisted it, hard. Anyone else's leg would've cracked, but Evolet now realized something he'd begun to suspect with the blow to the jaw.

Zaire's leg didn't crack, and he swung it unexpectedly, with such force that Evolet lost his grip and flew against the hard wall.

Zaire wasn't like him. He wasn't like Jason, either. He was... "Hyper-T5," Jason had called it.

Evolet's jaw hurt more than anything else ever had. But of course. Nothing and no one had ever been able to hurt him before.

Before T5.

Zaire didn't lose a moment before pouncing, this time for real. He dragged Evolet to his feet and looked hard at his dazed expression before slamming him against the wall again, this time by the shoulders, with a strength that nearly knocked the fifteen-year-old unconscious. There was a dent in the wall.

Zaire let him crumple to the ground, and then gripped him by the shoulders again, intending to repeat the tactic.

Evolet's eyes flew open, and as he was lifted off the floor he kicked out madly, attacking Zaire's strong hold with desperately working fingers. Zaire ignored it at first, but then Evolet kicked him in the stomach, hard, and Zaire grunted in anger and pain. Which was more than he'd gotten out of Evolet. Thus far, Evolet had somehow kept his mouth shut.

But that changed when Zaire moved his hands to Evolet's neck and held him against the wall, his feet off the ground, his fingers tightening relentlessly.

Evolet found himself gasping for air as he kept struggling, though he was slowly getting weaker. He had already been seeing stars when his head smashed against the wall, but this was a different kind of faintness.

He couldn't breathe. His head was pounding.

He needed air, now.

Moira. Jasmine.

Evolet felt himself going limp. He couldn't keep fighting, but he kept his arms and legs moving feebly—uselessly. The surge of adrenaline was nearly gone by now. Like every other human, and superhuman for that matter, Evolet had to breathe. And Zaire knew that.

Mercilessly, the man kept pressing. It got easier and easier as the seconds ticked by—minutes to him, hours to Evolet.

Zaire began smiling again as Evolet stopped fighting completely and his eyes closed.

Waiting for the last signs of life to die away, Zaire was so absorbed in his deadly work that he knew nothing of any third presence until that presence poked him with a rough, stick-like rod made of twisted power cables.

Literally. Even if there was no real idiom involved.

The sensation was slightly disconcerting, but Zaire was more concerned about someone else being around than he was about the wires touching him. He let go of Evolet as a matter of course, and turned to see who it was.

He got a glimpse of a tallish, blue-eyed, angry-looking brunette, one wearing a Victor uniform despite looking very different from the average Victor. But that was all he got time to see before she touched the other end of the wires to the end of a large car battery.

The next thing he knew he was on the ground, helpless, and the girl was running over to Evolet, shouting his name.

"Evolet! *Evy!*"

thirty-eight

eanwhile, Conner and Violet had discovered Zaire's trap—in the worst way possible to discover traps: by being caught, hook, line, and sinker.

Zaire's men had almost succeeded in getting the two into a room on their own before they realized what was going on and refused to be pushed. Now they were in the doorway, fighting desperately not to be locked into a room where they couldn't do any damage.

Conner was only too aware of the fact that they were running out of time. It was about eleven-thirty, and they had half an hour left to stop the rocket from going off. Conner knew that Jason had said they had to wait till the very last minute, when things were starting to settle down and they might have a chance—the Base was impossibly busy during the day—but really, this was cutting it too close. If they even made it at all.

But Jason had asked Conner and Violet to distract the Victors. Conner comforted himself with the thought that that was exactly what they were doing—if tackling a whole crowd of Victors counted as distracting, which Conner sincerely hoped it did. Even though the Victors couldn't really hurt him or Vi, it was still exhausting to be constantly fighting slightly weaker superhumans who had one goal in mind: to get the two into that room and shut and lock the door. They were doing such a good job of it that Conner was getting worried they might actually succeed. And then, what would happen to the distraction?

He glanced at Violet while he shoved someone away from him almost without thinking about it. She was fighting in a businesslike way, as was typical of her, leaning against the opposite door frame. But there was a literal flood of Victors, and it didn't look like their ranks were going to run out anytime soon.

Conner sighed. They should definitely split up, and now.

"Vi, you really ought to get out of here," he shouted over the noise that was inevitable in a fight like this. But he figured he was wasting his breath.

Just as he'd expected, Violet shook her head vigorously. "No way, man! I'm staying with you and anyway these suits will keep everything out. Violet Army proof," she added, grinning.

He sighed, ignoring her ending remark. "I didn't mean it like that. But we should split up."

Violet was stubborn in her refusal. "Nope. But if you wanna go, lead the way. I'll follow—we're sticking together, Trooper!"

Conner shrugged. "Let's go, then."

He followed his own suggestion, leaping suddenly to the side and into the midst of their attackers. Not that they weren't expecting it—they were perfectly capable of hearing the conversation. But gradually Conner and Violet began making their way down the dark hall. Together.

* * *

"Evy! Evolet!" Jasmine was screaming in her brother's face as the sparks from the battery behind her died away. She was so scared. His face was so white, despite the forming, ugly bruise.

But he wasn't waking up. She took him by the shoulders and shook him—violently.

His eyelids flickered open for a moment, and she stopped shaking him, hoping he was finally waking up. Nothing happened for a few seconds, and she was about to start shaking him again when he opened his eyes, fixing his gaze on her face.

Jasmine smiled weakly, suddenly exhausted from fighting as well as overwhelmed with relief.

Her brother stared blearily up at her from his position on the concrete floor, an unusually sleepy look in his purple eyes. Or was it the goggles?

Jasmine couldn't tell. She pushed them up onto his forehead, ignoring the fact that the light source on them was thrown off track. No, his eyes really *were* cloudy. And he wasn't looking at her, but at the ceiling.

"Evy!" she yelled in his face. "Wake up! Or I'm going to tell Dad!" she added, as a last resort.

Evolet moaned, and his face twisted in agony. Jasmine held her breath, suddenly remembering how Riley Fletcher had died.

What had that man done to her brother?

Her own face twisted, and for a moment she thought she was going to cry. She held her hand over his left chest, trying to feel a heartbeat.

It was there. She glanced back at his face with renewed hope.

And the next moment her hand flew off his chest as he suddenly almost doubled up, coughing spasmodically. He sat up from the force of coughing. He coughed until she thought he was going to cough out his lungs. But finally he stopped, and leaned weakly against the wall, breathing heavily.

"Evy?" she asked for what seemed the millionth time. And he seemed to hear her, for his purple eyes focused on her face. Much to her relief, he smiled—a damaged smile.

"Jaz," he breathed.

And now she really was crying, but happy tears, not sad ones.

"I got lost," Evolet went on in a raspy voice, taking in his surroundings. It hurt to talk, and he winced as he felt a terrible headache coming on. "And I, umm—"

"Shut up," she interrupted hastily, "you sound like a throttled duck—"

"I am," Evolet mumbled.

"—Which means stop wasting your breath," she finished obliviously, and then completely undid what she'd just attempted by asking: "How'd you get lost?"

"Oh, I dunno," Evolet muttered, his voice getting stronger gradually. "I just did. What did you do with Zaire?" he questioned in turn, touching the back of his head gingerly.

"I shocked him—" Jasmine looked around, and suddenly realized that Zaire had disappeared, leaving the wires and battery behind. Her eyebrows shot up.

"What?" Evolet murmured. He was still watching her.

"He's gone," she admitted, waving her hand in front of her older brother's face to make sure he was still responsive. He was looking sleepy again, she noted unamusedly.

"Stop that," he growled, swiping at her hand with one of his own. She smirked but acquiesced.

"What do you mean he's gone?" Evolet asked a moment later, with an obvious effort.

She shrugged. "I dunno. He was there a few minutes ago. No, seconds ago," she insisted, correcting herself.

"Then you should—" Evolet began, unaware that his father had been saying pretty much the same thing.

Like her mother, Jasmine shook her head stubbornly. "No, we stay together. You'll get lost again," she added pensively.

"No, but if he's escaping, you have to warn the others, and I'll only slow you down," Evolet pointed out dryly. "Besides, we're winning, right? I'll recover here and catch up with you later."

She was clearly hesitating. "But—"

"Mom and Dad—and Jason—need to know if Zaire is getting away," Evolet urged.

Finally she stood up. "Fine. I'll go tell them."

"Wait," Evolet broke in quickly, just as she was turning around, "what time is it?"

"The time? Eleven fifty-two. Man, it's almost midnight," she realized as she checked her watch. "Hopefully Jason's done his thing already. Okay, Evy. See you soon."

"See you." He managed to wave after her, and then he let his hand drop limply at his side. He watched as his younger sister darted off down the hall, illuminated by the goggles' beams.

Like her brother when he was paying complete attention, Jasmine had a remarkable sense of direction, and now she used it as well as the keychain flashlight on her belt to find her way out of the seeming maze. She held a dart gun in the other hand, ready for anyone she might run into.

But as luck had it, the first person she met was Moira. She didn't know it was Moira at first, as her aunt was carrying a powerful flashlight that shone in her eyes and blinded her temporarily, but then Jasmine shouted and Moira lowered the flashlight, relieved to see that it was only her niece.

"Jaz!" Moira rushed over to her. "What's up? Where are Evolet and that—Jason person?"

"Evolet's resting—he got sorta hurt," Jasmine explained quickly, passing over Evolet's injuries briefly because she knew Moira would become extremely worried if she said anything more than that. "I dunno where Jason is—I was going to look for him, and Mom, and Dad."

"Conner and Vi are that way," Moira pointed behind her. "I didn't stick around because I don't see how I can help—they're dressed for fighting, but I'm not really. I dunno why I'm in here," she muttered, "I was only supposed to call the police. But whatever. We Whytes get sucked into things. Are we going to help your parents, then?" she finished, out of breath.

Jasmine half-shrugged, half-nodded, trying not to grin too hard. "Yeah, I guess," she returned.

They started off together. As they approached the sounds of fighting, Jasmine suddenly stopped.

"Do you hear something?" she asked Moira quickly.

Moira stared at her in bewilderment. "Umm, no, just your parents yelling to each other, and battle sounds in general," she admitted. "What, can you hear something?"

Jasmine held up a hand for silence, and then a moment later, she nodded, starting off again. "Sirens, I think. Police, maybe?"

"Perfect!" Moira approved enthusiastically. "Now we can finish up here!"

thirty-nine

Evolet was still sitting where Jasmine had left him, recovering slowly but steadily. He just wanted to go back to sleep. His throat hurt, his chest hurt, his jaw hurt, his stomach hurt—everything hurt, but above it all he felt like his skull had been smashed. Not a very pleasant feeling, especially for a teenager who'd never really felt pain before. It didn't take him long at all to decide he wasn't interested in feeling it again any time soon.

He couldn't sleep now—his head hurt too much—but after a few minutes of resting he became aware that he felt cloudy and lightheaded. Anyone else might have dealt with it as if it were a side effect of being literally smashed up—which it very likely was—but Evolet wasn't used to the feeling, and he didn't like it.

The air smelled strange. Maybe not strange to the average person, but strange to him. Immediately he thought of the rocket, and his heart skipped a beat.

Were they too late?

No. They couldn't be.

Somehow, he got to his feet, and picked up the goggles, using them to see both ways down the corridor. He saw where the fumes were coming from right away. They were seeping out from underneath a heavy door towards the end of the hall.

Desperately, he took off his jacket, holding it over his mouth and nose in the hope that it would filter some of the toxin out.

He crept over to the room, the feeling of faintness partly going away for the time being. Finally finding the doorknob, he threw it open; he was shocked, but not too shocked, by what he saw.

There was no roof to this room. The floor and walls were made entirely of concrete; against one of the walls, a backup generator was running. There was no one else there. But that wasn't what really caught his attention.

In the middle of the room—or courtyard?—was a rocket tower, mounted with a small, clear canister of some orange liquid. Around it were some thin plastic supports, and underneath the actual rocket, but Evolet noticed that the canister was leaking onto the ground, and that that was where the fumes were coming from.

And a foot or so away from the rocket was a control panel with a small display screen. It read *2:08.*

Evolet watched it for a moment, then froze as he realized it was actually counting down. Why hadn't Jason stopped it yet?

Should he go in there and stop it himself, or would the thing kill him? He didn't feel like dying, even if he was feeling somewhat injured.

But then, he told himself, if he didn't stop the timer, he *was* going to die.

They *all* were. Everyone was. Well, his family, at least.

So he had to.

Resignedly, Evolet began walking towards the control panel, being careful to step over the chemical spill.

And now he was too close to the fumes for his jacket to be helpful, he realized as the dizzy feeling came over him again with twice the force. How he got over to the timer, he never knew, either presently or afterwards. But get there he did, and he stared at it a moment, swaying. There were words written under a couple of switches. After a few seconds, they came into focus, and he could read them.

He found the *Cancel* button and hit it with all his tired strength. And then he flipped the *On/Off* switch. He was falling over, he knew it.

But before he did, he kicked at the wires from the control panel to the rocket. There were sparks, and something fizzed.

He found himself on the ground after that, his jacket not over his face anymore.

He didn't care. He *couldn't* care.

Everything was so peaceful. He was just going to go to sleep. It wasn't that bad after all.

* * *

Ever since Jasmine had succeeded in putting the power out, Jason had been looking for Zaire. He knew the rocket couldn't launch without electricity, and so he was certain that it was adequately disabled—he didn't know about the backup generator. But he did know that whatever Zaire would be doing, he would be working to fix the problem, and quickly.

Jason was rushing through the hallway near the rocket for the fifth time in the past half hour, when suddenly he heard something he hadn't before. It wasn't something turning on. It was something turning *off*.

He stopped, noticing the fumes by the door for the first time. Quickly, with a hurried glance at his watch, which told him it was thirty seconds to midnight, he dashed over to the door. It was ajar, and he pushed it open, half-expecting to see the final rocket preparations past the point of no return.

Instead, in the faint beams from his flashlight, he discovered that the timer was off and that the connection between the rocket and a backup generator was completely smashed.

Jason started stepping carefully over to the rocket to see where the fumes were coming from, but not carefully enough not to trip on an unnoticed limp form on the ground and sprawl face-down onto some liquid on the floor.

Stifling a shriek, the young man scrambled away, wiping off his face hurriedly while aiming his flashlight at the floor.

He was startled to see Evolet lying there, only too obviously unconscious. Close by him was an orange-tinted spill from the rocket, and then across the boy's outstretched arm was his purple jacket. There was a deathly white pallor to his face, and his mouth was half open.

Jason caught his breath. He'd seen death before. And this looked uncommonly like it.

The orange spill was the toxin, Schwann2. Evolet had breathed in the fumes, and still was—if he was even breathing at this point.

Jason was breathing the chemical, too. He felt himself getting stronger by the moment.

But right now he was worried about Evolet. Was it too late? But if it was, it was Jason's fault, and he knew it.

Quickly he sprang forward, and picked up Evolet and his jacket, grunting under the fifteen-year-old's weight and stumbling out of the room with him. He managed to get him a few hallways away, what with his newfound strength, but then he had to leave the teenager on the ground, while he inspected him anxiously.

At the same time, Jason felt uncommonly powerful. His blood was racing. And he didn't know whether that was a bad thing or a good thing.

Evolet looked a mess, with a bruised face and neck, and a huge bump forming on the back of his head. It looked like he'd been smashed against a concrete wall.

But Jason wasn't concerned about that right now—he was more worried about the effects the toxin would've had on his nephew. It was supposed to attack the T4 in his blood, which would naturally produce extreme heat—but Evolet's body temperature was normal. So there hadn't been a reaction— unless entire minutes had passed since the process.

Somewhat heartened, Jason proceeded to feel around for a pulse. He finally found it at the back of Evolet's neck and at the wrist. So he was still alive— theoretically. Jason hadn't exactly taken any medical classes.

But he wasn't breathing. He was so awfully still. And his pulse was getting weaker. Jason stared at the boy desperately, wondering what to do. He knew that if he went to go get help it would probably be too late.

A memory flitted through his head. Years ago, he'd fallen in a body of water somewhere. He didn't remember where; he'd been about five or six. But Petyr had pulled him out. Jason hadn't been breathing anymore at the time. But he could remember waking up to find his older brother pushing periodically on Jason's chest until the little boy's lungs started working again. That was it—

Working swiftly in his desperation, Jason did the same thing on Evolet, as close as he could get it. He shouted in relief as Evolet suddenly started coughing and breathing as well.

Finally the boy's eyes flew open—just when the lights came back on. Jason glanced upward, surprised.

Evolet was looking at him weakly. "Uncle Jason?" he wheezed. "You look different."

"I—I do?" Jason stammered, taken aback.

Evolet managed a nod. "Yeah... Your eyes are gray...brown... I dunno." He coughed so hard, he almost sat up.

Jason pushed him back down gently. "Hey, stop talking. Take a break. You look beat up."

The teenager opened his mouth to say something regardless, but suddenly they both heard a door opening some distance away, the one opposite the rocket room.

Jason glanced up.

forty

It was Zaire. Behind him were Petyr, Flynn, Tina, and others. They all stopped and stared at Jason and Evolet, who were about halfway down the hallway.

Zaire muttered something under his breath, pulling his dart-gun off his belt and shooting it at Evolet.

Instinctively, Jason stuck out his hand just in time to shield the boy's face, and the dart stuck in it. He froze. He hadn't realized what he was doing.

But the next moment, he realized that, after his Schwann2 exposure, the darts couldn't hurt him more than a tiny sting.

Brushing the V-feathered dart out of his hand, he stood up, blocking Evolet from the Victors' view. He stared hard at Zaire, noticing suddenly that Zaire's eyes were no longer a coral color.

Zaire had also exposed himself to the Schwann2, Jason realized. And with that realization came the knowledge that only he could match Zaire's strength now.

So it came down to this. Only one of the two could win this fight for their respective causes. A scarred, tested leopard-wrestler—and a twenty-year-old, inexperienced young adult.

Jason's hands grew nerveless as he stared at his opponent. Zaire stared back, realizing the same thing that Jason had.

This was between them now. No one else. And they both knew it.

The others with Zaire knew it, too. Petyr and Flynn were looking at Jason, and now Petyr smiled slowly, shaking his head.

"You win, Jason," he whispered before anyone else could say anything.

"We look out for each other." And Flynn nodded.

"I'm with you," Tina interjected quickly. And the next thing Jason knew, his siblings and Tina were fighting the other three with Zaire.

They carried the fight down the hall, back towards the door they'd come through. But Zaire and Jason were left there, Evolet behind Jason, though Jason knew he wouldn't be much help. The boy was too far gone for that.

Suddenly, with a snarl, Zaire leapt forward. Jason stayed right where he was, but stuck out his foot at the last moment, sweeping the heavier, older, and tougher man off his feet. Zaire toppled to the ground, grabbing Jason's legs and pulling him down as well. Jason let himself go down and twisted suddenly, ending up on top of his antagonist. He swung away at Zaire's face as hard and as fast as he could, knowing he only had a limited amount of time.

They fought each other fiercely, for all each one was worth.

One moment Jason was on top, and the next moment it was Zaire's turn. Zaire was breathing hard and fast, while Jason was literally panting as he kept fighting with everything he had.

But suddenly Zaire got to his feet, a despairing look in his dark-again eyes. He kicked Jason away from him, and as Jason had a brainwave and reached for the real gun at his belt, Zaire turned and fled down the hall. Away from the rocket. The enemy leader had given up.

It was then that Jason realized his siblings had beaten their antagonists. The three Victors were on the ground, out cold—"taken care of permanently," Flynn assured Jason as she and their older brother walked over to the seeming winner of the day. Tina stayed behind, almost abashed.

"He's just...left?" Jason murmured, hardly able to believe what he was seeing and hearing.

Petyr nodded. "Looks like it. We'll have to chase him—what's happened to you? Which reminds me, how did you beat him like that? He dosed himself with Schwann2."

"Yeah, I think I did the same thing," Jason admitted, touching a cut on his face absentmindedly. "Petyr, come help me with Evolet. He breathed that stuff in."

They went over to the teenager, who was unresponsive again. Petyr, a professional doctor—or professional in comparison with Jason—found his pulse immediately, and reported that it was extremely weak.

"You said he breathed in Schwann2?" he demanded. "And this is Evolet Whyte, right? That means he's done for."

Jason shook his head in disbelief. "No, he can't be done for, Petyr! He stopped the timer just in time, and he wasn't dead a few seconds—minutes—no, seconds ago. Come on, we can save him, right?"

It was Petyr's turn to shake his head. "There is no cure against T4."

"No—but—" Flynn broke off, dropping to her knees to look at her nephew more closely. "Petyr, fix him up. It's our fault he's like this. If we'd just decided to go along with our original plan—"

"Flynn, I'm serious, there is no way to fix it," Petyr broke in. "It's impossible. Completely impossible."

"What's impossible?" came a new voice.

The three Foleys looked up, towards the doorway, to see Conner, Violet, Moira, Jasmine—and a whole squad of police.

Petyr stood up quickly, brushing off the front of his Victor uniform self-consciously. "Hey, Whytes. I—um—"

"We're on your side now," Flynn interrupted calmly. "But Evolet is right here. And Petyr says he's done for—"

"Shut up," Petyr hissed. "You don't have to put it like that."

But the damage was done, and the four Whytes were already running over to where the boy lay, surrounded by the Foleys.

Violet was the first there, the other three following her. But Violet picked Evolet up first. She knelt, and held him sitting up as she looked at his face anxiously.

"Evolet?" she demanded anxiously, noting with a pang of remorse her eldest son's bruises. "Evolet!"

Moira stood behind her, not yet crying but with a look of deathly strain in her face.

Conner looked at Evolet once, then away.

He closed his eyes. He should have been there for his son.

And Jasmine held her older brother's hands, struggling bravely against the tears. She didn't want to cry. She'd already cried. And she'd already gone through the horror of thinking her brother was dead. It wasn't fair. Especially if he really was dead this time.

"He's breathing," Violet realized. "His heart is beating, too. He's still alive. He's alive," she said again, as if she had to convince herself.

Petyr's face was gray. "Yeah, but—"

Flynn elbowed him sharply. "Let's go clean up the mess," she suggested quietly. Petyr and Tina nodded, and they marched down the hall towards the rocket room. Jason glanced after them, a look of doubt coming over his face, and he jumped up to follow them.

Moira was still staring at her nephew, but now she shut her eyes tightly as the tears broke loose. She was praying the hardest she'd prayed in her life.

She couldn't handle this. If she were to lose Evolet—*no.*

"No," she breathed, opening her eyes and looking at Evolet again.

Her heart skipped a beat as she thought she saw his eyelids move. Just the tiniest bit.

Moira dropped to her knees now, unconsciously shoving Jasmine to the side. Violet was still holding Evolet, but Moira brushed the boy's longish dark brown hair out of his face, thinking to herself subconsciously that he needed a haircut.

"Evolet," she whispered, tracing his face with her fingers. Like she'd done when he was a baby.

He had been such a cute baby, Moira remembered.

Suddenly his face twitched, and his eyes flew open. They were vague and cloudy for a moment, then went back to their normal purple selves as he gazed around at his parents, aunt, and sister. But Conner's, Violet's, and Moira's eyes were closed, and only Jasmine noticed.

"Evy!" she exclaimed in unspeakable delight and relief.

And everyone else looked then, at the fifteen-year-old who was smiling weakly at them, his head in his mother's lap.

Violet bent down and wrapped her arms around him, hugging him so tightly that he felt that even his T4-ified ribs were going to crack.

He gasped for air, and finally she realized she was squeezing him too tight.

She loosened her hug—only for him to be smothered by his dad, aunt, and sister all at once. Finally, things calmed down, everyone crying happily.

"You're wearing my jacket," Violet finally noticed, smiling at Evolet through her tears.

"Yeah, you left it home, so—" Jasmine began, anxious to keep her brother out of trouble for something she'd done herself. As if he was going to get into trouble *now*.

"No, it's my old jacket," Violet realized. "You know what, Evy, you keep that."

He grinned back. "Thanks. I think I like it."

"I can't believe—" Moira stared at her nephew incredulously. "It's a miracle."

"There are things that science can't explain," Conner began, trying to sound wise. His older sister gave him a look to freeze fire.

"Evolet, if you die again, I'm going to really kill you," Jasmine broke in, feeling angry and overjoyed at the same time.

Evolet winced. "I died?"

"No, no, no," Violet shook her head. "Nobody died. We're all alive here."

He smiled up at her—and remembered something. "Mom, was there ever a time you called me 'Little Trooper'?"

forty-one

The excitement among the Whyte kids didn't die down for months. Even in June it was still being discussed. And on June 9, Charles's birthday, Evolet and Jasmine reviewed the details for what must have been the millionth time. They were doing it in their favorite place for that sort of thing, too: a tall office building roof in Annapolis.

"At least Uncle Jason is going to be back in time for the party tonight—supposedly," Jasmine added doubtfully. "But I hope he will be."

Evolet nodded. "Yeah, Dad said he's flying in at four—"

"I heard," Jasmine interrupted. "Anyway. I'm glad he dealt with Zaire."

"It wasn't just him," Evolet laughed. "Aunt Moira said a bunch of the U.S. Army went, too. But he's taken care of now, thankfully."

"Why'd he go to Africa?" Jasmine wondered.

Evolet shook his head. "I dunno. But I think Jason said he's African."

"Oh, yeah," Jasmine remembered. "I guess it makes sense, then."

Her brother checked his watch. "It's almost three-thirty. We'll have to go to the airport soon to pick up Jason."

"We have a few minutes longer," Jasmine returned, leaning back almost lazily.

"Why do you always do that?" Evolet wondered.

"Do what?" Jasmine questioned, glancing at him confusedly.

"Lie back on the roof like that. Isn't the metal sort of warm?" Evolet wrinkled his eyebrows.

Jasmine laughed. "Yeah, but who cares? I wish the pool got this warm."

"Ha, I know, right?" Evolet grinned. "But maybe it will be next Sunday.

Dad said we can go in after Mass, and brunch—"

"I know, I know," Jasmine interrupted airily. "Why do you think you have to tell me everything?"

"I'm talking to myself," Evolet grumbled sarcastically.

Jasmine didn't catch it. "Isn't that a sign of insanity, or something? Oh, but what am I saying?" she went on before he could reply. "Everyone already knows you're insane. Signing emails *Trooper A2*—"

"Mom likes it," Evolet interjected heatedly.

"She thinks it's cute." Jasmine rolled her eyes.

"Oh, shut u—" Evolet broke off as he realized she was kidding him.

The thirteen-year-old crossed her arms. "It's not fair, anyway. Why can't *I* be Trooper A2?"

Evolet shrugged. "Well, everyone knows I'm braver and stronger and smarter than you—"

"*Not!*" she shrieked, nearly shoving him off the roof.

Adjusting his position, Evolet went on obliviously. "Well. I take that back, I guess. But I'm still the eldest."

"Eldest means nothing," Jasmine snorted.

"Anyway, if it's cute, then why do you like it?" Evolet asked pointedly.

She smirked. "Because I'm a cute little girl, that's why!"

Evolet couldn't keep from laughing, but he shook his head hopelessly. "You can be Trooper A3. How about that?"

"Not the same," she sniffed. "*You* can be Trooper A3."

Evolet threw his hands in the air. "Are you kidding me!" he exploded. "That makes no sense at all!"

Suddenly both of them jumped, and Jasmine nearly slid off the slightly slanted roof as they heard a new voice behind them.

"You're both Troopers, you two. Stop fighting. There doesn't have to be just one."

"Mom!" the teenagers squealed, turning around quickly to see Violet on the apex of the roof, grinning down at the two of them.

"It's time to go," she laughed at their surprise. "Moira was going to call you in, but I decided to go and find out where you guys are all the time." She looked around and nodded appreciatively. "Nice place here. Tree house?"

"Tree house?" Evolet echoed. "I dunno. It doesn't look like one. More of a lookout."

Violet clicked her tongue. "That's right. Maybe you two should build a *real* tree house this summer. In an actual tree."

"M—o—m!" Jasmine protested. "Tree houses are for babies!"

Evolet's eyebrows shot up. "I never had one," he muttered, but Violet was ready to move on to more urgent topics.

"I need to wash your jacket, Evy," she told him, putting her hands on her hips in her businesslike way.

"Okay!" Obediently, the boy started peeling off the purple jacket. He didn't usually wear coats during the summer, but he'd been surprised to discover that his mother's old jacket was actually made of some strange, insulating material that kept him perpetually cool. He loved it.

"I didn't mean *now*," Violet laughed, but she caught it anyway when he tossed it at her. "We have to go," she added, more seriously, tying the jacket around her waist.

"Beatcha both home!" Jasmine yelled. She was already making her way down the extremely dangerous side of the building.

"Cheat!" Evolet howled after her in dismay.

His mother grinned at him. "There's another way to do this, you know," she told him, and he blinked.

"How?" he demanded candidly.

She winked. "Follow me."

He stood there on the roof, gawking in astonishment as his mother retreated to the very edge of the roof and took off at a run. Crossing the roof in no time at all, she jumped, flying across the short distance between this roof and the next—and over the terror-inspiring drop between them—with amazing agility.

She landed on the edge of the second roof, pulling herself up to it and standing up. Turning, she glanced back at Evolet, who was frozen still with his mouth hanging open.

"You coming?" she shouted to him over the sounds of traffic from the streets below. "We gotta hurry if we're gonna beat Jaz!"

"I—I'm coming," Evolet stammered, suddenly discovering how to move again. Taking a deep breath to calm his nerves, he got to the end of the roof like Violet had. Then he started running. By the time he made the awful leap, he was going even faster than Violet had been.

He was shocked by the brief, weightless moment of sailing through the air. He'd jumped before, but nothing like this. It was amazing.

Exhilarating. Breathtaking.

And then he was on the other roof, and he landed hard, grabbing hold of the apex before he rolled off and down the dizzying side of the building. He picked himself up, shaking his head to get his thick hair out of his eyes. He looked up to see his mother smiling confidently at him.

"Got it?" she asked quickly. "Yeah? Let's tackle the next one together."

And so they did, roof after roof. Run after run. Jump after jump. Evolet's pulse was racing, but he felt like he could do this all day. He was getting the hang of it. And apparently Violet was already an expert at it.

They were a few streets away from Moira's house now, where the public buildings ended. It was no trouble at all to slide to the ground from here—the roofs were much shorter. Evolet looked down the street and laughed himself to tears as he saw Jasmine running desperately towards Moira's house. He and Violet took off for the final stretch, Violet laughing as well.

"Cool, huh?" she asked her eldest, who could only pant and nod furiously in answer at this point. "But don't you ever tell your dad. Got that?"

He had to collapse on the porch. It was too much. He was laughing fit to burst. Violet giggled too, shaking her head in despair at his fit of hilarity.

"He's crazy, right, Mom?" Jasmine leapt up the steps, panting, an almost Alison-like scowl on her face as she saw that Evolet was already there. "Cheaters. You cheated!"

"You don't even know what we did," Evolet managed, and his younger sister's face broke into a helpless grin.

"Not yet," she had to admit. "But I will!"

"Drink some water, both of you," Violet cut in, suddenly getting serious as befitted her, an adult. "And then we're leaving," she added as she headed inside, untying the jacket. "So, be in the car in two minutes."

Evolet and Jasmine glanced at each other, mischief sparkling in their eyes. "Right!"

They dashed inside. Smiling, Violet followed, taking the purple jacket to the laundry room.

Her face got serious again once she was alone, and she unzipped the jacket pockets, feeling inside them. Her hand came back out holding two small, purple vials.

She stared at them a moment and clicked her tongue, dropping the vials into her own pocket and feeling in the other one of Evolet's. There was nothing there. She checked them both again. They were both empty; there had only been the two vials.

Violet shook her head, frowning. She thought she had saved three. No, she was *sure*.

She checked the pockets again, then ran her hands across the linings of the jacket.

Nothing. Maybe she had imagined it. It had been twenty years, after all.

Sighing, she shrugged, zipping up her own pocket with the vials inside. Then she stood up, dropping Evolet's jacket into the washer.

Maybe there had been three vials at one point. But now there were only two.

Hopefully enough.

If she ever needed them.

THE END

epilogue

People stared at him as he walked by, gazing down at the ground and muttering to himself incessantly. But they weren't going to bother him with that leopard at his side. Maybe he was a leopard trainer; maybe he was an escaped lunatic. The police could deal with it. The average African wasn't going to risk his life bothering someone with a leopard.

Still, he looked extremely weird and out of place. He did look like an African, with dark skin and dark hair. Except that sections of his hair were a shocking, albino white. And his eyes were coral.

But what really got people's attention were the purplish scars on his face and arms. It was just too weird. People didn't scar that way—not *purple*. The marks had to be tattoos...though strange tattoos.

The man's eyes roved back and forth, and when he met another passerby's eye, he stopped and stared. They backed away in horror. There was a fiendish light in his coral eyes that filled anyone with terror. But once they stopped staring at him, he ignored them, intent on his business. Whatever that was.

As he spoke, his left hand was buried in the leopard's fur, rubbing its neck in a rough, fond way. The big cat purred almost constantly, a deep, deadly rumbling in the back of its throat.

"Stupid kids," the man was whispering under his breath. "Stupid kids, stupid school. Idiots! But they all dead."

He shook his head fanatically. The leopard growled in agreement.

"They think they be strong? Hah!" The man laughed in scorn. "We see. They know nothing. Even if they go to fancy American college." He bit his lip. "But we, you and I, Giza and Ayan, we need boat. Big boat. Big ocean, so big boat. And food. And then we go."

The leopard, whose name was apparently Giza, growled again appreciatively. Ayan smiled horribly.

"Those kids, we teach them lesson," he went on. It seemed he was always talking to himself—24/7.

"Showoffs," he spat. "Idiots. Giza and Ayan show them. They dead," he repeated himself. "But first we need boat and food."

His mind made up, he leapt ahead suddenly, the leopard following him. Ayan tore down the street, shoving past people who scrambled out of the way as fast as they could.

Forget leopard trainer. This man was obviously a maniac.

The two made their way to a butcher's stall, where Ayan jumped up onto the counter. The man staggered backward, staring in shock and alarm, with very obvious thoughts of calling the police.

Ayan kicked the man's cellphone off the counter, where it shattered on the roasting African pavement, and the butcher forgot that idea. But people in the street were already making the call for him.

"Want—cat food," Ayan told him obliviously, in broken, French-accented English, staring at the man with a giant grin on his face.

The butcher slowly began to recover his nerves, though he quailed under Ayan's ghastly stare. "C—cat food? They sell it at the pet shop. I dunno," he blurted out.

Ayan shook his head pityingly. "Noo, I mean big cat food. Like this" and he signaled to Giza, who joined him upon the counter, his tongue lolling out hungrily.

The butcher nearly fell over all over again, and made a weak gesture of putting his entire stall at the maniac's disposal. "A—any of that," he began waveringly. "Y—you can have it all."

Ayan ignored him then, glancing around the stall. His eye fell on a large package of mutton, and he grabbed it, bowing deeply to the butcher and making a dramatic exit by somersaulting backward onto the ground. He and his leopard shot down the street together, heading for the dock.

Once there, Ayan and Giza paced up and down the various piers until Ayan discovered a boat that he estimated was large enough and sturdy enough to carry him and his pet across the Atlantic Ocean. It was brand new, too, with the name *Waterflier 2052*. Ayan decided he loved it.

The boat's owner was aboard, but if that was a problem it was resolved when the madman and his big cat sprang aboard the boat without an invitation.

The short, timid fisherman took one look at the two—the wild and dangerous-looking leopard, and the package-carrying, scarred, coral-eyed, patchwork-haired Ayan—and decided it was time to go swimming.

He got ashore safely and ran towards the town, waving his arms in the air and screaming in Afrikaans at the top of his lungs.

Ayan paid him no more attention, instead turning his thoughts to loosening the boat from the dock. He noticed the fishing tackle on the deck and decided he'd figure it out when he got hungry.

"We go!" he shouted jubilantly to Giza a few minutes later, having discovered the mechanisms of the sleek, modern engine. "America, *we come!*"

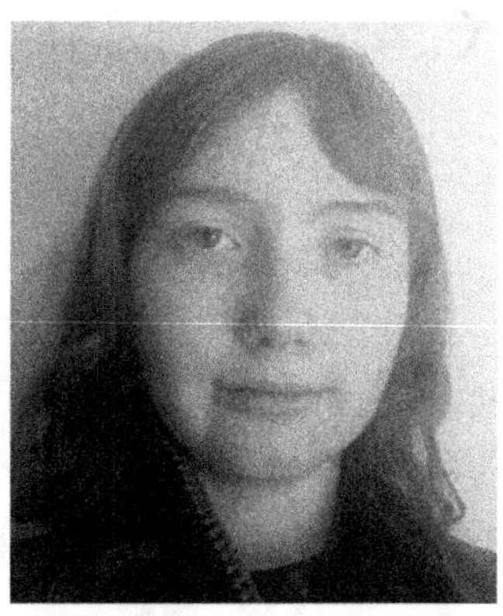

About the Author

Gabrielle Marie Kozak is an American author whose fiction explores pressure, endurance, and the cost of refusing to surrender oneself to oppressive systems. Her debut, *The Trooper Series*, began as a body of work written before she graduated high school and introduced her recurring focus on individual sovereignty under strain.

The eldest of nine children, Gabrielle spent nearly two years as a religious sister before turning her attention fully to writing and publishing. Her stories center on those who carry responsibility, those who break beneath it, and those who survive when systems fail.

She lives in Nebraska and loves writing, coffee, and all things Poland.

Website: **gmariaek.com**

Also by Gabrielle Marie Kozak

Thank you for reading!

If this story stayed with you, I would be grateful if you'd consider leaving a short review. Reviews help books like this find the readers who need them.

Your time, your attention, and your support truly matter.

If you'd like to continue reading my work, **The Trooper Series** is the best place to start.

Trooper A1: The Purple Blitzkrieg is the first book in the series.

Trooper A1: The Purple Blitzkrieg
SHE LOST HER BROTHER - JUST NOT THE WAY SHE THOUGHT.

Moira Whyte refuses to believe the **bloody evidence** that confirms her brother's death. Instead, she begins to hack into **Encephalon**, the underground network built to **subjugate the entire world.**

She's right. Her brother isn't dead.

He's worse than dead.

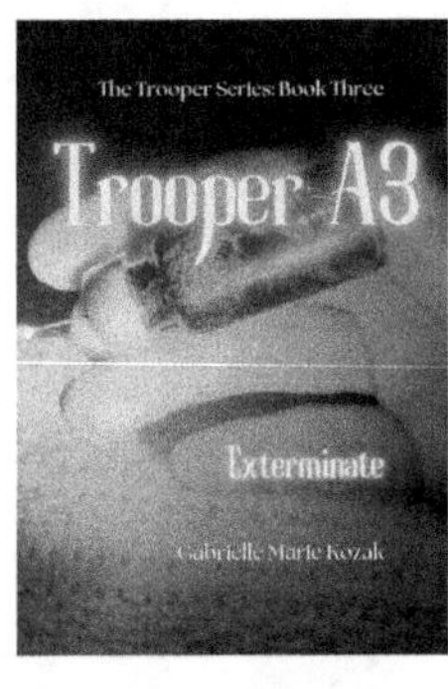

Trooper A3: Exterminate

SHE DIDN'T CHOOSE MOTHERHOOD—BUT RESPONSI-
BILITY CHOSE HER.

From a **college campus** to a **Texan laboratory**, Jasmine Whyte is beginning to realize that her **adult life** isn't going to be the peaceful future she fought for as a teenager. **Old ghosts** and **new threats** would like nothing better than to **tear her** from **her dreams**—and **her family.**

Jasmine isn't a mother. But there are children who **need her help.**

And she can only help them by letting them into her **own broken life**.